THE
GRAND MANUSCRIPT

Book 2 of The Papyrus Trilogy

Zoran Živković

The Grand Manuscript
Copyright © 2012 by Zoran Živković

FG-RS0022L4
ISBN: 978-4-908793-26-4

Cover: Youchan Ito, Togoru Art Works

Neoclassic Fleurons font
    used with permission of Paulo W–Intellecta Design

Cadmus Press

cadmusmedia.org

THE
GRAND MANUSCRIPT

Book 2 of The Papyrus Trilogy

Zoran Živković

Translated from the Serbian
by
Alice Copple-Tošić

Cadmus Press
2017

Contents

I PARKED THE CAR in the only free spot in the small parking area outside the building at 12 Oak Street. The name had surely been chosen by someone with a sense of humor. There were three trees on the short street: two lindens and a chestnut. When I got out of the car, my head was filled with the fragrance of a nearby flowering linden whose crown was bathed in the glow of the streetlights. A warm wind rustled its broad leaves.

I made for the entrance to a five-story building with a flat roof. Since it was not even nine-thirty, most of the windows were lit up. Lamplight was interspersed with the grayish, flickering radiance of television screens. Little eddies of dust and scraps whirled about the asphalt.

As I approached the entrance, a light went on in the foyer behind the glass door and a short, plump woman appeared. Since the light came from behind her, I was unable to get a good look at her face.

"Inspector . . . ?" she asked, opening the door a crack.

"Inspector Dejan Lukić," I replied. "Good evening."

The door opened wide and the woman moved aside to let me in. Now I could see her better. Although she had a youthful appearance, she was certainly over forty. Her short red hair was cut in a bob reaching just below her prominent double chin. Large thin-framed glasses and full bright-red lips filled her round face. She was wearing what seemed like a colorful poncho over her beige blouse. Her dark skirt reached below mid-calf, and her plain black shoes had low heels, although one would have expected them to be high. A large leather briefcase hung from her left shoulder.

"Good evening," she said after closing the door behind me quickly. She held out her hand. "Miss Ljubica Aksentijević. Literary agent."

I did not expect such a firm handshake from a woman of her size.

"So we are colleagues," I said with a grin.

She raised her eyebrows. "Colleagues?"

"Agents."

"Oh, that. I never liked that title. It sounds too. . . ."—she pondered briefly as though looking for the right word—". . . .inaccurate. There's nothing police-like in my work. Quite the contrary."

"Nevertheless, our paths have crossed." She seemed to hesitate about replying to this and then let it drop.

"Excuse me for not waiting for you outside. The wind shatters my nerves."

I nodded. "It does that to lots of people. Even when they are indoors. On windy days people act more strangely than usual."

"It has no effect on you?"

"Not much."

"That makes me feel a bit better. If the wind bothered you like it does me, I'd feel bad if it turned out that I've summoned you in this weather for no good reason."

"Don't you worry about that. It's always best for everyone when it turns out that the police have been summoned for no good reason."

The corners of her mouth lifted briefly. "I hope that's the case here too. Although. . . ."

If she had intended to finish the sentence, she was interrupted when the light in the entrance suddenly went out. Had I not moved, or had I looked for the switch on the left-hand wall, nothing would have resulted. But I reflexively turned to the right—and the collision was inevitable.

First her "Oh!" was heard in the dark as her head collided with my shoulder and then my "Excuse me," accompanied by a brief groan as her heel smashed the toes of my left foot (had she been wearing high heels, she would have made a hole in the casual shoe), followed by her "Sorry." Finally, the light came back on.

We stood there for several moments in silence, filled with unease, avoiding each other's eyes. She rubbed her right temple with the tips of her short fingers and I barely held back from inspecting my trampled foot.

"Let's go," she proposed at last. Without waiting for my agreement, she circumvented me and headed for the elevator at the far end of the foyer. To left and right were other glass doors leading to apartments on the ground floor.

Thanks to mirrors on three walls and the ceiling, the elevator looked considerably more spacious than it actually was. When she raised a finger to press the button for the fifth floor, I was disconcerted to see the same movement multiplied all around me. For a moment I couldn't tell which was the real person among all the likenesses. I wasn't even sure which one of me was real.

The confusion must have shown on my face because she smiled.

"It's even more unpleasant when you ride alone. I avoid this elevator when I'm not with someone else. I prefer the stairs, even though I'm in no shape to climb them. I'm all out of breath after seventy-two steps. But that's how it is with smokers. You don't smoke?"

"No."

"Of course. A police inspector has to be in excellent shape."

"Most of my colleagues smoke. Some are even chain-smokers."

"Then how do they handle stairs?"

"They use elevators whenever possible. Not even psychedelic ones put them off."

She opened her mouth to reply, but there was no time. The elevator stopped smoothly and the door opened at my back almost without a sound. I hesitated a moment and then stepped out backwards. Had I tried to turn around in the cramped quarters, we might easily have collided again.

She came out after me and gestured toward her right. "This way."

Before following, I glanced the other way. The elevator was in the middle of the corridor. Two doors faced each other at the far end. The opposite side was the same. The floor was covered with thick dark-red carpeting and each wall had four red drawings on a white background at regular intervals; at a fleeting glance they did not seem to show anything specific.

Miss Aksentijević stopped at the left-hand door. There was a peephole between two plaques. The upper one was small and plastic and bore the number 19, and the lower one was large and made of metal and had nothing written on it because there was no need. The shape of the plaque was sufficiently articulate. Would anyone but a writer have chosen the trademark of a stylized goose quill dipped in an ink pot?

It took a while for Miss Aksentijević to dig a set of keys out of her briefcase. It consisted of at least fifteen keys of various shapes and sizes. And then a full minute passed before she found the one she was looking for.

"Here it is," she said contritely, handing it to me. The set jingled under the key. "See for yourself."

I slid the key into the lock. It entered about halfway. I pushed harder but it would go no further. I tried to turn it left and right, also with no result. I took it out and inspected it. It seemed all right to me.

"Are you sure it's the right one?" I asked.

"Absolutely. I always remember where I keep each key. It's seventh from the end."

I looked at the key ring that held the set together.

"From which end?"

"From the left," replied Miss Aksentijević self-confidently.

I turned the ring over in my hand. What had been on the left was now on the right. I waited for her to say something, but she remained silent.

"Would you mind if I tried a few more keys?"

"Go ahead, but I'm certain. . . ."

She didn't finish her sentence because we were plunged into darkness a second time. It was darker than in the entrance hall. Down below a quantity of light from the street poured in through the glass door. Even though the window at this end of the corridor was large, it looked onto an unlighted area and was not much use.

Both of us might have reached for the nearby switch on the wall, but after the embarrassment we'd experienced five floors below, we stood stock-still, each waiting for the other to turn on the light. One of us would have done it eventually had something not snapped at our backs. Then a deep, menacing growl filled the corridor.

∽ 2 ∾

I turned around at once. I felt Miss Aksentijević brush against me, squeezing as far as she could into the narrow space between my back and the door. She mumbled something unintelligible and grabbed my left bicep.

It was not complete blackness in front of me. The lights were not on in the neighbor's apartment, but a weak glow came through the open door and outlined the vertical rectangle. It did not seem artificial which meant it probably came from a window somewhere in the background. The center of the dimly illuminated door frame was filled by the outline of a tall, thin figure standing on the threshold. The growling came from near its legs.

"I would advise you to keep still," rasped a male voice. "Even the slightest movement will trigger Adam and he is a dangerous dog."

Miss Aksentijević's grip tightened even further. She repeated something in a low voice but I still could not understand.

"There is no reason for Adam to attack us," I said, trying to appear unruffled. "Our intentions are not at all dishonest."

"Except that you're trying to enter a stranger's apartment."

"It's not a stranger's. . . ." objected Miss Aksentijević, but I interrupted her.

"There's a good reason for it."

"No doubt. That's what all burglars think."

"How dare you. . . ." came a raised voice behind my back. This time the sentence was left unfinished because the growling increased.

I placed my hand over hers on my arm.

"We can easily prove to you that we're not burglars."

"Soon you'll get a chance to prove it to the police."

He raised his half-clenched right hand to his head.

"You don't have to call the police," I said. "The police are already here. I am an inspector."

The cellphone remained a little longer by his ear. Then he lowered his hand, and we fell into a brief silence.

"Show me some identification. But don't make any sudden movement. Whatever you try, you won't be faster than Adam. Even in the dark."

"Why don't you turn on the light? It will make it easier for all of us."

"Easier for you, sure. Adam and I don't mind it like this. So?"

I disengaged my hand from Miss Aksentijević's fingers, reached into my jacket pocket and took out my badge. I extended it forward slowly. I was certain that the growling would rise again, but the dog remained silent.

"Shall we turn on the light anyway?" I proposed once more, when he had taken the badge. "You'll see better."

A quarter of a minute passed before he replied. "You can see with your fingers too and you don't need light to do it, Inspector Lukić."

The dark outline moved slightly to the left, the switch sounded and the lights went on in the corridor. Miss Aksentijević quickly let go of my arm and put her hand over her mouth, but a sigh of relief slipped out nonetheless.

The tall man with the large German shepherd in front of him seemed even more elongated by his long black smoking jacket. His wide-collared shirt and the scarf around his neck were also black. Had he been dressed more cheerfully, I would not have thought he was over forty-five, but in this get-up he seemed ten years older. His thick salt-and-pepper hair was pulled back in a ponytail. His face was thin with regular features and a high forehead.

The most remarkable thing about him was his eyes. The jade-green color seemed to shine from within. Never before had I seen such eyes in a man. But in spite of their brilliance, his eyes were empty, unfocused, looking somewhere off to the side of us.

"Sorry," said the man, raising the badge in the direction of my voice. "I had no way of knowing that you were an inspector."

"Of course you didn't," I replied, taking the badge. "Its not easy to recognize a police inspector even when . . . it's not dark."

I stopped myself at the last moment from saying—". . . .even when you can see." I had no experience of talking with the blind.

"Is something wrong with Miss Jakovljević?"

"We hope everything is all right."

"If it were, would you be here so late with her agent?"

"How do you know. . . .?" said Miss Aksentijević without finishing the question. She was no longer standing behind my back, but was still next to the door, her eyes mostly fixed on the dog.

"I don't forget a voice. I heard you when you came before."

"Do you eavesdrop on your neighbors?"

"I don't have to eavesdrop. I have acute hearing and those who can see usually talk needlessly loud."

I got the better of Miss Aksentijević, who had already opened her mouth to say something. "Voices do not reveal professions. How did you know she was an agent?"

"Voices reveal more than you imagine, Inspector. If you know how to listen, of course. But I didn't reach this conclusion from her voice. I found out from Miss Jakovljević. She mentioned you."

"Really?" Miss Aksentijević's voice was a mixture of surprise and displeasure.

"If you recognized the voice of Miss Jakovljević's agent, why did you think it was a break-in?" I asked.

"I had my reasons."

"What reasons?" asked Miss Aksentijević sharply.

The jade eyes turned toward her. Not past her but straight in her face as though he could see her. And even more—see through her. The man, however, did not reply. Tense silence surrounded us.

"Forget about that now," I said, breaking it finally. "When did you last. . . ."—even though I did not say "see," the pause gave me away—". . . .hear Miss Jakovljević?"

His head turned toward me and his eyes turned blind again. "The day before yesterday. She dropped by to see me on Wednesday evening. We had a little chat. I didn't hear her after that."

"Do you mean, she didn't drop by anymore?"

"Not only that. The door to her apartment hasn't opened since then."

"That's what I told you. . . ." interjected Miss Aksentijević. She was no longer bristling, as though suddenly changing her opinion of the blind neighbor's acute hearing.

"You might have missed it. It could have happened when you were asleep."

"I did not miss it. I sleep very lightly. Miss Jakovljević is still inside."

"Oh, please do something." Miss Aksentijević's voice had regained the hysterical tone it had had when she called the police a little over half an hour ago. I had had to take great pains to calm her down.

"Thank you for your help, Mister. . . ."

"Teodosijević. Branislav Teodosijević."

He held out his hand, but before I had a chance to shake it, we were plunged into darkness again. I stood there bewildered, uncertain what to do. He could not know that the lights had gone out, and if I tried to turn them on, the dog might attack me. He had been good-natured enough while there was light, but my ears were still ringing from his growling in the dark.

Just as I concluded that the best thing would be to propose that Mr. Teodosijević push the light button by his door again, he did it without any prompting. As though replying to my puzzled look, which he could not see, he said tersely:

"Three minutes and forty seconds."

I thought of asking him whether the blind had an acute sense of time too, but did not have the chance because he had extended his hand again. The tiny hand of Miss Aksentijević gave a stronger handshake than that of Mr. Teodosijević, although his was almost twice the size.

"Inspector Dejan Lukić. Nice to meet you. Please forgive us for disturbing you."

"Nice to make your acquaintance, even under such circumstances, Inspector Lukić. I'm sorry if Adam frightened you."

"He didn't," I lied. "It's the same with policemen as it is with doctors. People usually meet them when there's something wrong. I hope this will turn out to be harmless."

He seemed to search briefly for the proper reply and then said, "If I can be of any assistance. . . ."

"Thank you, but there's no need." I paused briefly, then added, "For now."

"Then I'll be seeing you."

He turned, let the dog go in before him and then returned inside. Once the door had closed with a click, my eyes were drawn to the brass plaque under the peephole. It was also without an inscription: in the form of a painter's palette.

∽ 3 ∾

Miss Aksentijević shook her head and sighed, then turned toward Miss Jakovljević's door.

"Please hurry," she said and, still upset, motioned with her chin to the keys in my hand. "Something must have happened to Jelena . . . Miss Jakovljević."

Before I started examining the keys, I thought of a way to prevent the problem that awaited us in about two minutes.

"When the lights go off again, please turn them back on."

A smile briefly softened the anxious expression on her face. She nodded.

Of the sixteen keys, five fit the type of lock. I tried them one after the other. Three would not go in at all and only two got in halfway through the hole.

Even though I knew it wouldn't work, I tried to turn them.

"None of them is the right one," I said.

She took the set of keys briskly from my hand and selected the last key I had tried.

"Of course it is," she said angrily. "This is the key to Jelena's apartment."

"Maybe it is. But it does not open the lock."

"It clearly does not open the lock. Because it is locked from the inside and the key is in the lock. It doesn't take a highly insightful inspector to draw that conclusion."

Now I was the one to sigh.

"Highly insightful inspectors avoid drawing rash conclusions."

"Rash? This couldn't be more obvious."

"In my line of work you quickly learn that what is obvious does not always have to be right."

Impatience joined the anger on her face.

"Instead of having this pointless discussion, you should break into the apartment as soon as possible. That's why I called you, after all."

"Then you should have called a burglar. Although he would have had a hard time saving you from Adam. The police don't break into apartments without a strong reason. We only do so once we establish that it really is necessary."

"Isn't it here?"

"Not necessarily. Let's assume that you are right and it is locked from the inside. That still does not mean that something is wrong with Miss Jakovljević. She simply might not want to open the door."

She looked at me in disbelief. But before she had time to answer, we were surrounded by darkness. From the thud that was heard I would say she hit the switch with her fist.

"Hogwash!" she almost shouted. "Of course

she would open the door for me. Why in the world wouldn't she?"

"Maybe she's writing and does not want to be disturbed. Writers are often like that."

"How do you know what writers are like?" She did not even try to hide the disparagement in her voice. "I'm certain you don't meet them very often in your line of work."

"We meet all kinds of people. But there are other ways to get to know writers. By studying literature, for example."

She eyed me suspiciously.

"You studied literature?"

"You would be surprised to learn all the things police inspectors have studied. I know of one, for example, who studied paleolinguistics. The science of the languages of the oldest human communities."

"I know about paleolinguistics," she said, offended. "But what's the use of literature in police work?"

"To help an inspector properly handle a case like this, you might say."

She stared at me for a few moments. Her eyes showed that she was hunting feverishly for a comeback.

"Well, Inspector," she said at last, "here is proof that you are not handling it very well."

She reached inside her purse again, rummaged around a bit and then took out a cellphone. She pressed several buttons nervously with her thumb. She did not bring it to her ear but held it in her hand.

"Listen," she said tersely and put her ear to the door. I did the same. A moment later, from inside the apartment there came the sound of a soft chirp that repeated itself at regular intervals. She did not hang up until the eighth ring, as though wanting to be completely sure I had heard. Then she returned her phone to her purse and looked at me in triumph.

"Would a writer who doesn't want to be disturbed

leave their cellphone on? And the landline is also on, I checked."

"Probably not," I agreed. "But this opens up a new possibility."

"What new possibility?"

"A writer who did not want to be disturbed would not have a telephone with them."

She wrinkled her brow. "I don't understand you."

"Miss Jakovljević left her cell at home because she did not need it wherever she withdrew to write in peace."

"But she didn't go anywhere. She's in the apartment. You heard Mr. Teodosijević."

I lowered my voice almost to a whisper. "I got the impression that you don't trust him."

She glanced briefly at the neighboring door. If she had thought of replying to this, the lights going off again prevented her. This time the sound of the switch was barely heard.

"In any case, the door is locked from the inside," she said, also softly.

"What if it isn't?" I replied in a normal voice.

She looked at me briefly once again, without a word.

"It is. Didn't you just establish that yourself? The key won't go into the lock."

"That might be because it's the wrong one."

"It always worked before. How can it not work now?"

"The lock has been changed."

She started to shake her head. Her mouth was half-open, as though she wanted to say something, but some time passed before she finally spoke.

"Who changed the lock?"

"The only one who has a right to: the owner of the apartment. I assume that is Miss Jakovljević."

Another pause ensued.

"Why would she change it?"

"Because she doesn't want anyone to enter her apartment when she's not there."

"But that's ridiculous. I'm her agent."

"Writers might have secrets even from their agents."

"They didn't teach you much about the relationship between writers and agents in your literature studies."

"I don't recall they ever mentioned agents."

She bit her lower lip. The bunch of keys jingled in her hand. I thought she would explode for sure, but she kept her temper in check.

"Does that mean you won't do anything?" Her voice was trembling.

"I'll do the first thing that a police inspector has to do before he does anything else. I will try to establish the facts. Are we unable to unlock the door because it is locked from the inside or because the lock has been changed? And to establish that, I will need the help of a burglar."

"Burglar?"

"Former. Inspector Tanasije Vesić was a virtuoso burglar before he became a policeman."

"Do the police employ burglars, even former ones?"

"Only if they've never been apprehended and sentenced. The police did everything they could to pin something on him. He drove them crazy with his exploits, but all their efforts were in vain."

"Even so, he was a thief and there's certainly no room for thieves in the police force."

"He never stole anything."

She looked at me, puzzled.

"What kind of burglar doesn't steal? So why did he break into places?"

"He couldn't resist the challenge. He chose only the most difficult and famous locks. Not a single one remained unpicked. He wasn't at all interested in what was behind the door. He would just move something inside as proof that he had opened it. That was his trademark."

"Oddball. But what's the good of having him join the police?"

"Enormous benefit. It's always better to use a gentler procedure than brute force. Like here, for example." I nodded my head toward the door in front of us. "In particular because he'll know in a moment whether the key is in the lock. And if it is, there will be no need to break down the door. Which is quite unpleasant, by the way. He will open it quite elegantly."

"So have him come at once."

"Not all policemen are on call around the clock, Miss Aksentijević. I don't think Inspector Vesić is on duty tonight. I'll have to check."

"But this is urgent. Something might have happened to Jelena!"

"I don't want to seem callous, but if something truly has happened to her, I'm afraid we are way too late to be of any assistance. You should have called us a lot earlier. Please excuse me for a moment."

I removed my cellphone from the inside pocket of my jacket and moved down the corridor.

"But how could I. . . ." Miss Aksentijević started to say behind my back. She was interrupted by the darkness once again. I took another two steps, stopped and waited for her to turn the lights back on. But this did not happen. I thought with a sigh that I would have to search for the switch on the wall, then remembered that this was not necessary. I pushed one of the buttons on the phone at random. The screen lit up and I looked for Vesić's number on my contact list.

Less than a minute later I headed back towards Miss Aksentijević. My eyes were already adjusted to the darkness so I was able to see her plump outline against the weakly lighted window at the end of the corridor.

"I'd say we've had enough of playing hide-and-seek," I said, making peace.

About ten seconds passed before the lights finally went back on. As I walked toward her, reproving eyes shot daggers at me, but she did not speak.

"We're in luck. Inspector Vesić will be here in about forty minutes."

"Forty minutes?"

"He lives way over on the other side of town. Even if he used his flashing light, he would only get here at most six or seven minutes earlier."

"What'll we do here for so long?"

"We don't have to stay here. In the end we would alarm the entire building by constantly turning on the lights, and I'm sure you wouldn't like us to remain in darkness all that time."

"Would you like it?"

"I'm used to waiting in even worse conditions than darkness, when it can't be helped. But that's not the case here."

"So, where shall we go? It's not much better down in the foyer where I was waiting for you to arrive and it's really windy outside."

"On my way here I noticed a café-bar not far away, just around the corner. We could wait for Inspector Vesić there." I paused, then added: "We can go by car, if you like, although it's quite close."

She turned indecisively towards the door to Miss Jakovljević's apartment and then to the one across from it.

"Let's walk," she said at last. "My nerves are shattered enough already, so the wind can't do me much more harm."

A smile flickered at the corners of her mouth.

This time I got into the elevator first and turned to face her. As the doors began to close, I noticed something that I had missed on the ride up. I had probably been confused by the three mirrors around me and the one on the ceiling, so that standing with my back to the doors, I had not seen in the reflection that they were lined with mirrors too. I quickly lowered my eyes to the floor. Covered with the same red carpeting that lined the corridor, it was an island of reality surrounded by infinite illusion. I left the elevator slightly dizzy.

The wind dispelled it as soon as we exited the building. Miss Aksentijević bowed her head and drew the poncho around her. Whirlwinds played about our feet. After passing through the conical glow of the streetlight next to the linden, I looked briefly at the building. Seven steps later I stopped and looked at it again.

I did not reply to Miss Aksentijević's questioning expression, but continued toward the café-bar. There was no need to upset her, particularly since I was not even certain myself. Perhaps I had not paid close enough attention, but I would have said that, on my way there, the row of four windows on the upper left-hand corner had not been lit. Now a weak glow emanated from the last window but one.

$\backsim$ 4 $\backsim$

NOT UNTIL WE WERE already quite close did I realize that it was not a café-bar but a teashop. It was located slightly below street level. A wrought iron fence extended in front of two arched windows. Three tall steps led down to the entrance where a metal sign in the shape of a teapot hung above the door.

Herbal fragrances and semidarkness welcomed us inside. Banquettes covered in dark-brown leather lined three walls. Eight little round tables on spindle legs were placed in front of them, each with two round chairs. Subdued lighting came from behind screens along the cornices. Only the fourth wall with the bar facing the entrance was better lit.

The dozen customers were sitting mostly on the banquettes. I could only make out their shapes in the darkness. The melody of a stringed instrument competed with the din of voices. If the steam from the tea cups had been more abundant, I might have thought I'd stepped into an old-fashioned opium den.

Only two tables were free. I gestured toward the one in the far right-hand corner next to the window and Miss Aksentijević nodded, so we headed in that direction. She took off her poncho, settled on the banquette and placed it next to her, while I sat on the right-hand chair.

A large woman broke off her conversation with the man behind the bar and came briskly toward us. She had short, thick hair that resembled a yellow brush. Her brown dress, the same shade as the leather banquettes, was sleeveless, emphasizing her muscular arms. There was an older look about her, although she was probably still in her thirties. If she'd played sports in her younger days, most likely it had been the shot put or hammer throw.

When she reached our table, I noted a brass pin on her lapel in the same shape as the sign above the entrance.

"May I help you?" she said in an aptly deep voice. Her lips turned up briefly in the hint of a smile.

"Tea, please," said Miss Aksentijević.

The woman narrowed her eyes.

"Do you ever go to bookstores?" Her voice was effortlessly reproving.

Miss Aksentijević eyed her suspiciously.

"Sometimes," she replied warily.

"What would happen if you went into one and said, 'A book, please'?"

"This is not a bookstore," said Miss Aksentijević after another brief hesitation.

"No, it isn't. But it isn't an ordinary teashop either. You can't order just any old tea here."

"Then what should I order? You don't have a menu."

She gestured toward the little table that was empty except for a green ceramic teapot figurine. Dried flowers in a variety of colors sprouted out of the holes in the lid.

"We don't have one because it's not necessary. We concoct teas tailor-made to each customer."

"How do you determine the fit?"

"The customers usually help. They tell us what ails them."

"Then this is a doctor's office, not a teashop."

"Many of our teas are indeed medicinal."

"Well, there's nothing ailing me."

"Everyone's got something ailing them, even if they're not aware of it."

Miss Aksentijević's eyes began to flash.

"The wind bothers her," I interjected. "Do you have any tea that might help?"

As she answered me, the teashop proprietor kept her eyes on Miss Aksentijević.

"We have tea for every ailment."

"Wonderful," I said. "Then perhaps you could find something fit for me."

"What's ailing you?"

"Illusions."

The shot putter's head finally turned toward me. She looked at me in silence for a few moments.

"I'll see what I can do for you," she said at last.

She turned and headed back to the bar. Even though she was wearing soft-soled shoes, her steps echoed above all the other noises.

"I don't like teashops," said Miss Aksentijević dejectedly after the proprietor had left the table.

"We'll certainly be more comfortable here than waiting in the corridor. Besides, we won't be here for long." I paused and smiled. "And tea against the wind might do some good."

She looked at me dubiously.

"How can a police inspector be so gullible?"

"Don't underestimate tea. I've tried some that work wonders."

"They get rid of illusions?" she asked mockingly.

"That too."

"What are these illusions that are troubling you?"

"Police work is full of illusions, ambiguities. It's not all that easy to figure them out. What happened tonight is no exception."

"Is that so?" Her voice turned serious.

"Yes. I have several dilemmas. Perhaps you could help me get rid of one even without the tea."

"Which one?"

"When was the last time you saw or heard Miss Jakovljević?"

"The day before yesterday. We spoke on the phone Wednesday evening. I already told you that during our first conversation. Don't you remember?"

"How could I have forgotten? Barely an hour has passed since then. But people are usually upset when they phone the police, particularly if they don't know the person they're talking to, and so something important slips their mind. You didn't say whether you called her or she called you."

"I called her. Why is that important?"

"I'm trying to establish something. On her cell or home phone?"

"Home phone. She was at home, if that's what you want to find out."

"That doesn't necessarily mean that she was. She could have set it up so any call to her home phone when she wasn't there was transferred to her cellphone."

"But her cell is at home. You heard it."

"She might not have only one. The transfer can be heard by a change in the ring tone. Did you notice that by any chance?"

"No, I didn't," she said without a second thought. "You're barking up the wrong tree. Jelena certainly answered the phone from her apartment. That's the only place she could have been."

I looked at her inquiringly. "Doesn't she ever go out?"

"Rarely when she's writing. And when she's under a deadline, like now, she doesn't budge."

"Sounds almost like a hermit."

"Not almost—absolutely. It's only students of literature who imagine that writers lead a leisurely and exciting life. In reality, it's lonely and full of hard work."

"But not even hermits can do without the outside world. They have to get hold of food, for example. How does Miss Jakovljević get food supplies if she doesn't go out?"

"I brought her fresh food every other day."

"Literature studies deplorably underestimate the invaluable contribution of literary agents."

Miss Aksentijević pressed her lips together, but before she could say anything, heavy steps echoed once again. The teashop proprietor was carrying an oval tray with two steaming bell-shaped cups. She came up to us and set first the dark-green one in front of Miss Aksentijević and then the white one in front of me. The tea in my cup was reddish and in hers it was blue.

"I hope it has an effect," she said to me. "It isn't easy to deal with illusions."

"You're telling me."

She smiled as she turned to Miss Aksentijević.

"You certainly won't be bothered by wind anymore."

She turned at once and headed towards the bar so Miss Aksentijević was again unable to bluster in reply. All she did was push the cup angrily away from her, spilling some into the saucer.

"Won't you even try it?" I asked.

"You're to blame for everything," she said almost in a growl. "First you brought me to this awful place and then you even mentioned the wind to that . . . that . . . woman. See what it's come to."

"The only thing you complained about was the wind. If I were better acquainted with literary agents, I would know what else troubles you."

"Whatever it is that troubles us, tea certainly can't get rid of it."

"To be sure. That was just a promotional wisecrack. Try the tea, you might like it."

"How could I like something that is such a revolting blue? And in a green cup?"

"Would you rather have red tea in a white cup?" I asked, pushing my cup toward her.

She shook her head. "No, thanks. The life of a literary agent isn't easy, but at least we aren't troubled by illusions."

"Yes, illusions would certainly get in the way of grocery shopping. While we're on the subject, when was the last time you took them to Miss Jakovljević?"

She looked at me darkly for several moments before she replied.

"Wednesday about noon. I brought them today too at the same time. I buzzed the intercom but she didn't answer. At first I thought she was still sleeping. That would not be unusual. She stays in bed later when she has spent the night before working. I toyed with the idea of going up to her apartment and leaving the food, but I would have wakened her up that way."

"Didn't the buzzing of the intercom wake her?"

"She turns it off before she goes to bed. The telephones too."

"The telephones are not turned off."

"The intercom might not be either. I couldn't establish that by myself. If I had, I would have called you earlier."

"What did you do when she didn't answer the intercom?"

"I went home to put the food in the refrigerator. I called her by phone around two."

"The house number?"

"First the house number, then the cell."

"Did you think she'd gone out somewhere?"

"What else could I think?"

"Even though she was up against a deadline?"

Miss Aksentijević sighed deeply.

"We all have our breaking points. Jelena has had no trouble coping with deadlines until now, she's a real professional. But she's only made of flesh and blood."

"How do you think she would react if she reached that point?"

She shrugged her shoulders. "I don't know. At first I assumed she'd gone out for a walk. That would do the least harm. If she were to recharge her batteries like that, it would be easier to spend another night working."

"Wouldn't she have told you she was going out? Or at least answered your call?"

"Maybe she didn't feel like having to explain me. She knew that I would scold her."

"You would have scolded her?"

"That's my job. Do you know what some writers call agents? Especially the lazy writers."

"What?"

"Slave drivers."

I smiled. "I can imagine you with a whip in your hand."

"If only I could use that whip to drive lazy policemen," she replied, smiling in return.

"When did you suspect that she hadn't gone for a walk?"

"After seven. It was already getting dark. If she really had gone for a walk, it was high time she returned. The sooner she started writing the better. But she still didn't answer either phone. I consoled myself for a while, thinking that she was engrossed in her work and that was why, but I finally realized that she couldn't be ignoring all my calls. Why would she keep the phones on if she didn't want to answer them? And so, just before nine, I went to Jelena's apartment again. You know the rest."

I got to thinking.

"You didn't call her yesterday?"

"There was no reason. I didn't want to disturb her."

I indicated the white cup that was just barely steaming.

"Are you sure you won't?"

She shook her head.

I drew the saucer to me, raised the cup and took a tentative sip. The tea had a bitter and sour taste but I was unable to recognize a single ingredient. I found it pleasant. In two sips I drank almost half the cup.

Miss Aksentijević raised her left arm and looked at her watch.

"Just a bit longer," I said. "When is that deadline that's giving Miss Jakovljević such a headache?"

"Monday. My headache is worse than hers."

"Why is that?"

"It seems you really know very little about literary agents."

"You are the first one I've ever met."

"If the manuscript of the novel is not ready by Monday, I will be the one to face the publisher, not Jelena. That's an agent's primary duty, not buying groceries."

"Do you expect problems with the publisher?"

"Problems? I'll be crucified, that's what will happen to me. He'll ask to break the contract."

"Is that so terrible?"

She looked at me like a teacher would a backward pupil.

"Is it terrible? Not at all. We'll only have to return the large advance and then pay even larger damages."

"Both of you? Isn't the contract only in the writer's name?"

"It is. But there is also a contract between the writer and their agent. I get fifteen percent of the author's earnings, but I have to pay that same amount in case of non-fulfillment of the contract."

"That's rather unpleasant."

"I had to be ready to make concessions to become Jelena's agent. She's a very lucrative author. There aren't many like that, so my colleagues fought for her tooth and nail."

"Fifteen percent is still less than eighty-five percent," I noted with a grin.

"Little consolation. Do you have the slightest idea how much that fifteen percent advance and damages amount to?"

I shook my head. "No, I don't. I thought there wasn't much money in literature. At least that's the impression you get from lit classes."

She sighed once more, then waved her hand dismissively.

"Forget literature classes. That's not the real world. Jelena can certainly afford it, but I simply don't have that much money. I might even end up in prison."

"There's another similarity in our jobs," I said with a smile.

She looked at me, puzzled. A moment later, when she realized what I was referring to, she opened her mouth to retort, but I was faster.

"Can't the deadline be extended?"

She stared at me crossly a few moments before answering.

"We've already extended it twice. He won't agree to a third extension."

"Why did you let such a dangerous contract be signed when you knew that Miss Jakovljević is unreliable when it comes to deadlines?"

"She's not unreliable," said Miss Aksentijević, almost shouting. Two or three customers turned their heads towards us briefly from neighboring banquettes. Once the heads had turned the other way, she continued in a voice that was softer than necessary. "She never was before. Until this book. She would finish the books on time. Even considerably before the deadline."

"Why is the new book an exception?"

She shrugged her shoulders. "I don't know. From the very beginning everything about it has been somehow . . . unusual."

"Unusual?"

"Yes. To begin with, Jelena would always give me the manuscript to read while she was still writing it. She wouldn't let anyone else read it. This time, however, she won't let me either. Without any explanation. The only thing I know about the book is its title." She stopped briefly, as though thinking twice, then added: "*Find Me.*"

"Interesting title."

"Have you read anything by Jelena? Or are you like all those who study literature and have a high-handed prejudice against detective novels?"

"The first thing you learn when studying literature is to get rid of all your prejudices, particularly the high-handed ones, and then that there is only one essential division in fiction: good and bad. Many great works could be classified in the detective genre. That by no means stands in the way of their being great."

"But you haven't read any of Jelena's books?"

"There are a lot of books I haven't read. Luckily, it's easy to atone for such a sin. I will certainly read one of Miss Jakovljević's books."

"What a surprise it would be if you liked it."

"Why a surprise?"

"Because Jelena has recently started to lose faith in what she writes, even though it has made her famous. And rich. It's as though she's had enough of detective novels."

There was no time to reply to this because my cellphone started ringing in the inside pocket of my jacket. I took it out, told my colleague Vesić that we were on our way, then stood up.

Miss Aksentijević started to rummage through her

briefcase, looking for her wallet, but I gently took hold of her arm.

"Allow me. You might be facing bankruptcy, and every cent will be dear."

She hesitated briefly over what to say to this, then nodded her head with a grin.

"Thank you."

She put on her poncho and I quickly finished my tea. Then I went up to the bar, put a bill in front of the teashop proprietor and motioned her with my hand to keep the change. The response to this was also a smile. As before, it did not seem to suit the stern face.

"Might I ask you something?" I said.

"Inspector, isn't it?" she replied tersely.

"Is it that obvious?"

"No. You look more like someone whose field is literature."

"How did you guess?"

"By the way you drink tea."

"I had no idea you could tell someone's profession from that."

"And not only their profession, if you have a practiced eye."

"Would you recognize a writer too?"

"Artists are the easiest to recognize. They are my most frequent customers." Her gaze swept over the people in the semidarkness. "There you have three musicians, two painters, a sculptor and a writer."

I took a look at the banquettes along the walls, but was not even certain who was holding a teacup just then.

"Amazing," I said.

She bowed briefly. "Which writer are you interested in?"

"Miss Jelena Jakovljević. Does she ever come here?"

"Has something happened to her?" she asked in return.

"Everything's all right. I'm interested in her as a reader, not as a policeman. I love her detective novels."

"Really? Which one is your favorite?"

Her piercing glance seemed to plunge into my blinking eyes. The seconds drew out, hopelessly slow, which is what happens when you get caught in a lie.

When I finally answered: "*Find Me*"—I had the impression that someone else had said it.

Now it was her turn to blink. Then she nodded her head towards the entrance to the teashop.

"Your girlfriend's losing patience," she said in a low voice. "Come back another time when you don't have company."

∽ 5 ∽

AS WE DREW NEAR to the building, I took a good look at the façade. Fewer of the windows were now alight. All four on the upper left-hand corner were dark. There was no fear that Miss Aksentijević would follow my eyes as her head was bowed and seemed to protrude from a teepee.

Inspector Vesić was waiting for us in front of the entrance. Miss Aksentijević looked at him in predictable disbelief. Nothing about him reflected the conventional idea of a police inspector. And if there is a notion about the appearance of famous retired burglars, he would have had trouble fitting that too.

He looked like a polished businessman: graying hair, rather small stature, stout, with ruddy cheeks, round wire-framed glasses, a thin mustache above his upper lip, dressed in an elegant black suit with a dark-red bow tie and a hat. He was carrying an oversized briefcase with as many as three security locks.

He took off his hat and bowed as we approached.

"My respects, madam. Good evening, esteemed colleague."

"Miss," I said, correcting him. "Miss Ljubica Aksentijević, literary agent."

"Nice to meet you," she said. The smile softened her puzzled expression.

He took her extended hand but not to shake it. He bent over, brought it to his lips and kissed it lightly.

"Literary agent? How very nice to make your acquaintance. I might be in need of your services."

"Do you write?"

"Now and then. Lyric poetry."

"Lyric poetry?" Miss Aksentijević made no attempt to hide her disappointment. "I'm afraid there's absolutely no demand on the market for any kind of poetry right now. But if you had something along the lines of . . . a memoir. . . ."

Silence fell momentarily. Inspector Vesić threw me a quizzical look and I looked at Miss Aksentijević, also quizzically.

"The life of a police inspector," she hastened to add, rescuing us all from the awkward situation, "must be full of excitement. Detective stories are quite widely read. Both fictitious and real."

"Unfortunately, there's nothing exciting about my work. It's almost the same as a locksmith's. Nothing like a detective story." He paused a moment and then gestured toward me. "But if you're interested in really sensational detective stories that are also true, you have Inspector Lukić here."

"Is that so?" said Miss Aksentijević, turning toward me inquisitively.

"Yes," continued Inspector Vesić, "some of his cases outdo any and all fiction."

I gave him the same look he had just given me.

"My colleague is just joking," I said. "Look, this case is among the most exciting I've covered. And you tell me—who else would want to read about it?"

There was no reply. Her eyes went back and forth

from Inspector Vesić to me. Then she stuck her hand in her briefcase and took out some business cards. She handed one to each of us.

"Don't hesitate to call me if you decide to write something of your memoirs. I would be delighted to represent you as your literary agent."

"Perhaps this is not the most suitable moment for a business conversation," I said, taking the card and putting it in my pocket. "You're in a hurry, if I'm not mistaken."

"Of course," replied Miss Aksentijević with a ring of discomfort and then reached into her briefcase again for the set of keys.

As we entered the foyer, Miss Aksentijević and I hesitated. Inspector Vesić hesitated too and looked at us in bewilderment.

"After you," I said at last, nodding toward the button.

She smiled, then pushed it. We continued towards the elevator, leaving Inspector Vesić without an explanation.

All three of us watched in silence as the red numbers slowly changed on the small display above the door while the elevator descended. The fact that it came from the fifth floor did not have to mean anything special. No doubt somebody lived in the two apartments at the other end of the corridor.

It was not until the doors opened that I realized we had a problem. Had Inspector Vesić been slimmer we could all have fitted in, but as things stood it would be very tight. Who ever thought of putting such a cramped elevator in a five-story building? Particularly since there was plenty of room.

Miss Aksentijević was the first to enter. She stood with her back against the mirror on the far wall of the elevator. When Inspector Vesić went in after her and did not turn around toward the doors, she looked at me anxiously over his shoulder, realizing what would happen if I tried to enter too.

"I'll take the stairs," I said, sparing her grief.

She replied with a fleeting smile and Inspector Vesić, who was misled by the mirrors, turned around to see what was the matter. He had no chance to ask anything because the doors started to close that very moment. Miss Aksentijević clearly had not hesitated to push the button for the fifth floor.

A wide stairwell wound around the elevator with a brass handrail extending along either side. With my very first step I began counting the stairs. I had tried for a long time to get rid of this habit. I would switch my thoughts to something else, try to mix up the numbers, but nothing worked. Part of my consciousness always continued to count undisturbed. I finally gave up when it turned out that there was a benefit to this shortcoming. In my line of work it's sometimes useful to know the exact number of stairs.

Just as I was headed for the fourth floor, the lights went out. The stairwell had no windows so I was plunged into pitch blackness. I swore under my breath. Widening the elevator would certainly be too expensive now, but it wouldn't cost a thing to adjust the lighting timer to a longer interval. Three minutes and forty seconds were insufficient under ordinary circumstances, let alone in an emergency.

I could have continued since I knew there were six more steps to the landing, but I had no reason to rush. Miss Aksentijević would be pushing the button any moment. She was probably aware of my predicament. I felt for the handrail on the left and drew close to it. The seconds continued to draw out, however, and I was still stranded in the dark.

I had already decided to continue when I was suddenly filled with foreboding. Nothing external caused it. Nothing disturbed the impenetrable darkness, nor did any sound reach my ears. Nevertheless, I had the distinct impression that I was no longer alone on that short stretch of stairwell. Someone seemed to be rushing down the handrail on the other side.

I was uneasy, wanting to do something, but nothing suitable came to mind. At first I thought of stretching out my arms, but I might have lost my balance that way. And I didn't exactly feel like reaching for someone I knew nothing about. Would it be better to speak? While I was figuring out what to say, the lights came back on.

There was no one to be seen. I hesitated just a moment and then rushed down the stairs, reaching the ground floor in no time at all. But it was empty. I thought of going out in front of the building, but dropped the idea. If someone had opened the door, I would have heard it in the total silence. I looked around the foyer, wondering where else someone could have gone. The two glass doors leading to the apartments were closed. If they had been opened I wouldn't have missed that either.

And then something crossed my mind. What if I'd had the wrong impression and someone was going up, not down? It's easy to lose your orientation in the dark. I rushed toward the fifth floor, two steps at a time. I was already quite a ways up when I realized I should have taken the elevator. What if the lights went off again? No, there would be enough time, barely a minute and a half had passed since they had come back on.

Miss Aksentijević and Inspector Vesić were standing in front of the door to Miss Jakovljević's apartment. They stared at me in bewilderment when I burst into the corridor next to the elevator. I glanced briefly the other way and then headed toward them. But I stopped after the second step and turned my head toward the stairwell, peering in that direction a few moments.

Something had finally thrown the counter in me out

of kilter. What I had been seeking for so long was clearly a combination of excitement, haste and taking the steps two at a time. I had counted seventy-five and not seventy-two, the number of steps Miss Aksentijević had mentioned. I would have achieved that number too if I had continued my initial climb. From the first floor to the third there were four times nine stairs. There had to be the same number from the third to the fifth floor. Where had I miscounted, adding three nonexistent stairs? I shook my head and then continued down the corridor.

"Was someone chasing you?" asked Miss Aksentijević as I reached them.

"Ghosts," I replied with a smile.

"It took you a long time to climb up for someone being chased by ghosts. I could have got here faster myself, even without the ghosts."

"I would have got here faster if you hadn't hesitated to turn on the lights."

She wrinkled her brow. "I didn't hesitate at all. I pushed the button as soon as the lights went off. Isn't that right, Inspector?"

Inspector Vesić nodded. "That's right. Don't be taken in by the tricks of inspectors who don't stay in shape."

I gave him a hard look and then waved my hand dismissively.

"All right, forget it. Let's get down to business."

Inspector Vesić took off his hat and handed it to me. Then he interlaced his fingers, turned his hands palms outward and straightened his arms. His knuckles cracked. He shook out his hands and thrust his left hand into the inside pocket of his jacket. He pulled out two little round steel rods about fifteen centimeters long and as thin as knitting needles.

Those picks were the only tools he used. He never opened his briefcase, although he always carried it with him when he was on duty. He refused to reveal the contents, causing imaginative stories to be spun. All that was known for sure was its considerable weight. Should conjectures reach his ears, he would merely smile. His reply was that he would open his briefcase when he had to. There had been two or three attempts to open it without his knowledge, but no one had managed to get anywhere with even one of the locks.

Now he placed it on the floor next to him, lifted his pant legs a little and knelt down by the door. He twirled the little picks briefly between his fingers before inserting them into the upper and lower parts of the lock. Just as he started to move them ever so slightly, we were plunged into darkness.

I heard Miss Aksentijević rush over to the switch. It didn't take her long to feel for it on the wall. She was already quite experienced. When the lights came back on, the little picks were no longer in the lock.

"It's locked from the inside," said Inspector Vesić. "The key is in the lock."

"What did I tell you?" said Miss Aksentijević triumphantly, almost in a shout.

"Can you remove it?" I asked, disregarding her interruption.

"I can try," he replied. His calculations were always qualified. He never made promises and always kept them.

He reversed the picks and inserted them into the lock once more. Before getting down to work he closed his eyes. To a casual observer he might have appeared quite motionless. This petrified scene seemed to slow down the passage of time. I glanced at Miss Aksentijević. The little twitches around her mouth indicated her barely contained impatience.

When the lights finally went out again, the sound I heard made me think she had jumped as she headed for the switch. But before she had a chance to push it, Inspector Vesić's sharp voice stopped her.

"Leave them off!"

We remained in the dark. I wondered how he had known, without looking, when the lights had gone off. He must have been able to tell through his lowered eyelids. I had no answer to my other question: why did he prefer to work in the dark?

Now with our sense of sight excluded, time passed even more slowly. All that disturbed the silence was the periodic rustle at my back caused by Miss Aksentijević's fidgeting.

When the key fell to the parquet floor on the other side of the door, a sound that we would otherwise have barely heard, it seemed almost like an explosion. I started and Miss Aksentijević let out a choked "Ah!"

"Shall I unlock it or will you use the key?" asked Inspector Vesić in an even tone.

"We'll use the key," I replied. "Lights, please."

They were back on before I had finished my sentence. Miss Aksentijević started rummaging through her briefcase at the same moment. It was some time before she pulled out the set of keys. She tried to avoid me as she headed for the door, but was stopped by my outstretched hand.

"Allow me."

She stared angrily into my eyes for several moments but did not object. She opened her hand and let me take the keys. Inspector Vesić, who was already on his feet, moved a little away from the door. I handed him back his hat, then approached and started to search by memory for the five keys that fitted that type of lock.

When not even the third one turned out to be right, I was sorry I hadn't accepted his offer to unlock it with the picks. It would certainly have been faster. And then, finally, the fourth key made a full rotation along with a click.

I PLACED THE KEYS in the outside pocket of my jacket and then took latex gloves from the inside pocket and put them on. As I started to open the door, Miss Aksentijević drew close to me.

"Please wait here," I said to her, keeping the door closed.

"But I have to go in," she said adamantly. "Jelena. . . ."

"If something is wrong with Miss Jakovljević, you might not want to be inside."

She covered her mouth with her hand. "You think. . . ."

"There is no need for conjecture. I'll find out what has happened soon enough."

"Even so, I want to see. . . ." There was a ring of hysteria in her voice.

I looked at Inspector Vesić. He stepped forward and placed himself between the door and Miss Aksentijević, forcing her to take a step backward.

"Listen to the inspector," he said to her calmly. "Just be patient a little longer."

It seemed she would keep insisting, but nevertheless refrained.

I went inside quickly and closed the door behind me. I was in semidarkness. Faint streetlight filled a window that was four or five meters away. Little could be made out in that weak light. It seemed there was a short hallway in front of me that led to other rooms. There was the outline of a door in the middle on the right. It was ajar.

First I groped around the right-hand wall and felt a wooden surface under my fingers. It was ribbed, not smooth. Narrow vertical spaces separated sections that were about an inch wide. I didn't have to reach up to the hooks at the top to recognize a coat rack. I had one like it at home. Nothing was hanging on it.

I turned to the other side and felt for the switch, then had to squint when the entrance was illuminated by a strong light.

The window that had now turned into a dark oblong was flanked by the multicolored spines of books on shelves, and below it was a round glass table with metal legs and four metal chairs. To my left, next to the entrance, was another door, probably to the bathroom because there were three switches on the outside.

I went straight ahead and then stopped at the door that was ajar and peered inside. The strip of light from the hallway indicated it was a large room. Under the right-hand window was a large wooden desk with a monitor rising in the middle. As I slowly opened the door, the opposite wall entered my field of vision. It was completely lined with books except for the lower middle part taken up by a three-seater upholstered in dark-pink plush.

I entered the room and turned on the lights. This time I did not have to search for the switch. It had to be on the left because the door opened to the right. The light bulb in the yellow ceiling fixture was weaker than the one in the hallway. I turned around slowly. The layout on the right-hand wall was similar to the one facing me. Since it was shorter, a two-seater of the same color was all that interrupted the background of floor to ceiling books.

Bookshelves filled every free space on the wall with windows. The only place where there were no books was under the left-hand window. That space belonged to music: a stereo system and two speakers in the middle with a row of CDs above it and old-fashioned gramophone records below.

A large printer stood on the far right-hand corner of the desk and behind it on a wide board above the radiator was a brass flower pot resembling a pail. A rubber plant with large leaves blocked at least a third of the window. On the opposite end of the desk, a thin goose-necked metal lamp rose straight up from a round base and then arched forward so that its light fell upon the keyboard. Between the monitor and the printer there was just enough room for a white fixed telephone. I did not see the cellphone until I went up to the desk. Small and black, it was inconspicuous next to the equally black keyboard. I put my hand on the lampshade: it was cold.

The fourth wall had the fewest books. Two rows of shelves extended just below the ceiling. The door I had entered was the smaller of the two on that wall. The other was more than twice as big with a folding door that connected the study to the smaller room I had first seen from the entrance. Now I could see a wall of books rising proudly beyond the glass table. The only thing that interrupted it was a closed sliding door on the left. Kitchen cabinets could be seen in the gloom through the glass of the upper half.

Before I went in that direction, I paused to consider the central part of the study's fourth wall between the two differently-sized doors. Eight paintings in four rows completely covered it. They were in thin rust-colored frames with wide light-brown *passe-partout*. The paint-er had used only two colors on a white background. A preponderance of black only gave way to bright red in the middle. The arabesques did not depict anything recognizable, but they seemed familiar nonetheless. As my eyes passed from one painting to another, it struck me where I had seen them: the drawings in the corridor came from the same brush.

I entered the smaller room through the open folding door and turned around. The space above the door also had eight paintings, but what they depicted was quite clear. If I'd had a chance to see the enlarged covers of Miss Jakovljević's books before going to the teashop, I would have remembered at least one of the titles and would not have been caught off guard when the shot putter asked which novel I liked best.

I barely pushed the sliding door and it moved to the right smoothly and without a sound. It was less than two meters to the opposite wall. Cabinets covered its entire length, narrowing the space even more. Nothing about the kitchen indicated that it had been used. Here, as in the rest of the apartment, everything was neat and tidy. So much so, actually, that it almost seemed like no one lived there.

The windowsill, level with the kitchen workspace, extended into a little counter and next to it was a wooden chair with a back. The only thing on the counter was a book-stand.

I turned on the light next to the door and went inside. On the left, across from the refrigerator and sink, rose a wide, two-sectioned closet. I approached and opened the lower, larger part first. It was filled with women's clothing and there were several pairs of shoes underneath. Then I opened the upper part. It contained neat piles of bed linen. I stood there indecisively for a moment after closing the closet and then opened the refrigerator. It was empty except for a large green apple on the middle shelf.

I turned off the light and closed the sliding door behind me as I left the kitchen. Only one room was left. I turned right into the hallway and stopped in front of the bathroom. The indicators above the three switches were small, so I had to move closer. I pushed the right one and started to open the door, but it was still dark inside. As I looked at the switch, puzzled, the lights flickered and went on. The neon light in my bathroom also has this short delay before it goes on. The all-encompassing whiteness dazzled me; there seemed to be no other color in the bathroom.

To the left were the sink and a towel bar with two towels. There was nothing on the little shelf under the large oblong mirror. Next to the far edge of the mirror was a round metal holder fixed to the wall for the ceramic beaker with a tube of toothpaste and a toothbrush sticking out of it. To the right was a washing machine with a small cabinet above it and beyond it was the toilet with the lid lowered.

A white plastic curtain was pulled over the bathtub that stretched from one lateral wall to the other facing the door. Even though it was opaque, I stopped in front of it briefly, trying to catch sight of something. Finally, I took hold of the left edge of the curtain, pulled it slightly and peered behind it.

The bathtub was not completely empty. I pulled the curtain halfway, squatted down and looked at the yellow rubber ducky on the bottom. A good minute passed before I finally stretched out my hand and picked it up. It was almost weightless. I held it for a moment and then put it back in the same place. I got up and pulled the curtain closed, left the bathroom, closed the door and turned off the light.

As I walked toward the study to turn off the light, out of the corner of my eye I caught sight of something gleaming on the floor near the bottom of the coat rack. I shook my head. This should have been taken care of as soon as I'd entered. I bent down and picked up the key that Inspector Vesić had pushed out of the lock. I started to put it in my pocket along with Miss Aksentijević's keys, but then stopped. I would need it soon.

Standing at the door to the study, I scanned it once again, then turned off the light. Just as I reached for the switch in the hall, there was a sharp "ping" behind my back. It confused me at first. My cellphone has that same ring, but it was in my inside pocket, not somewhere behind me.

I turned around and went back to the study. There was no need to turn on the light again. I would have been able to find Miss Jakovljević's cellphone even without the light from the hall, with only the faint external glow from the window. I remembered its location next to the keyboard.

"New message" was written on the illuminated blue background under the number 23:01. I picked up the black telephone, but before I had time to do anything, the screen went dark. I turned toward the hallway. I could handle my cell even in the dark, but not this one.

Pushing a button at random, I brought the blue screen back to life. Then, following the instructions at the bottom of the screen, I pushed another button. The "new message" notice faded but the message did not appear right away. First the blue turned white and then two words slowly formed as though emerging from below the surface.

"*Find me.*"

⌒ 7 ⌒

I STARED AT THE writing for about ten seconds until the screen went dark. Then I continued to look at the telephone in my hand, musing. Finally, instead of putting it back by the keyboard, I slipped it into my pants pocket.

Before leaving the gloom of the study, I looked around it one more time. When I turned off the light in the hall, the darkness around me grew deeper. The window at the bottom of the small room had metamorphosed again and become the source of weak illumination.

Miss Aksentijević was standing right by the door, a clenched fist by her mouth and her eyes filled with fear. Inspector Vesić had an inquisitive look on his face.

I inserted the key in the lock, turned it twice, then took it out and put it in the pocket with Miss Jakovljević's cellphone.

"Why did you do that?" asked Miss Aksentijević in

bewilderment as I put the latex gloves back in my inside jacket pocket.

"Because there is no reason to leave it unlocked. There's no one inside."

"How can that be?"

I shrugged my shoulders. "I don't know."

"But there must be someone. The door was locked from the inside."

"That's right," I replied.

"Then how is it possible that no one's there?"

"I don't know," I repeated.

She shook her head. "You want to spare me, don't you? You don't want to tell me . . . the truth . . . about Jelena?"

"The truth is that Miss Jakovljević is not in the apartment. And neither is anyone else."

"That's impossible." Her voice became shrill. "I don't believe you. I want to see for myself. . . ."

She took a step toward the door but I blocked the way.

"Miss Aksentijević. . . ." I started, but her shout cut me off.

"Let me by!" She raised her hands to get me out of her way. "You have no right . . . I must go in. . . ."

I grabbed her by the wrists, holding them tighter than I would have liked because she started to put up a fight. I was spared from further difficulties when the lights went out. She stopped resisting as soon as we were plunged into darkness. I waited a little and then let go of her hands. Everything was quiet for a while and then the sound of the switch broke the silence.

"Please forgive me," she said, her head bowed. "I'm a nervous wreck. This is all too much for me. I thought you were lying to me. . . ."

"There would be no sense in lying to you. If something had happened to Miss Jakovljević inside . . . anything at all . . . I would have had to call a doctor right away. Those are the regulations. And I won't be doing that. There's no work for a doctor here."

"So why won't you let me go inside and see for myself. . . .?"

"Because no one is allowed to enter an on-site investigation without authorization."

"Investigation?"

"Yes. An investigation will have to be conducted. The case has become more complicated than it seemed at the outset."

"That might take some time. . . ."

"It might."

"But there is no time. . . ." She glanced briefly at Inspector Vesić. "I explained it to you. . . ."

"Are you thinking of the deadline? On Monday?"

"Yes," she replied as though making her case.

"There are two whole days until Monday. Quite a lot could happen in the meantime."

She looked at me for several moments without speaking.

"One thing could be settled right away."

I knitted my brows. "What?"

"If I could just use Jelena's computer for a few minutes . . . Even an unfinished novel might do the trick . . . I wouldn't touch anything else. . . ."

"I told you why you can't go inside."

"All right, all right. But perhaps you could. . . ."

Now I fixed my eyes on her.

"You don't seem too worried about Miss Jakovljević anymore."

"Of course I'm worried. But if she isn't in the apartment, then there's probably no reason to worry."

"Do you have any idea where she might be?"

She shook her head.

"I haven't a clue. But if she's pulled this stunt on purpose, which now seems the only explanation, then your efforts to track her down will be in vain. She's very clever. As befits someone who writes detective novels."

"I have no doubt that she's clever. But it takes more

than cleverness to leave an apartment locked from the inside. Isn't that right, Inspector Vesić?"

The Inspector looked at Miss Aksentijević carefully for a moment before replying.

"Quite a lot more. You need magic for that."

"Wouldn't you be able to do that?"

"I am only an ordinary locksmith, Miss, not a magician."

She opened her mouth to reply, but we ended up in darkness again. I was the first to speak when the lights came back on.

"Why would Miss Jakovljević pull a stunt? Particularly when pressed by a deadline?"

"Oh, you'd better not try to figure out what makes a writer tick. She could have come up with all kinds of things. To make me suffer, let's say."

"Why would she torment you?"

"Because that's what writers do to their agents. You had no idea, did you?"

"No, I didn't."

"Forget the idealized notions you have about writers. They're all sadists who take particular pleasure in torturing their poor agents."

"Who would have thought?"

"So, will you help me?"

"Do you mean, will I check Miss Jakovljević's computer to see if there is a file with the new novel?"

"Not just check but copy it for me. I would be greatly in your debt. Here, I have a flash drive. . . ."

She started to rummage through her large briefcase.

"I'm afraid that's impossible. I have no right to enter Miss Jakovljević's apartment and even less to copy something from her computer."

She stopped searching and looked at me archly.

"Didn't you already go in?"

"The first time it was feared that something had happened to her. Now the only justification would be the assumption that she has decided to torment her agent. A sadistic relationship with one's agent, however, is by no means sufficient reason to raid a writer's apartment."

"What about the investigation? Isn't there going to be one in there?"

"I have nothing else to investigate in the apartment. I have assured myself that it is empty."

"So where will you conduct the investigation, then?"

"I will try to find Miss Jakovljević. She, above all, could tell us how she left an apartment that was locked from the inside."

"If she's decided to hide, you'll never find her. I warned you."

"We'll see."

She gazed at me briefly in silence.

"So you can't do anything for me?"

"I will be doing a lot for you if I find Miss Jakovljević by Monday. She is the only one who can give you the manuscript of her new novel."

She glanced at Inspector Vesić and then turned her eyes back on me. Her pursed lips indicated she was racing to think up something else to try, but before she could get a word out the lights went off again.

"We have no reason to stay here anymore," I said, once she had banged on the switch. "Let's go."

I gestured toward the corridor. Inspector Vesić put an end to Miss Aksentijević's hesitation by waving his hand as well.

"After you," he said with a smile.

I opened the elevator door for Miss Aksentijević, then moved aside to let Inspector Vesić pass, but he shook his head.

"It's my turn to take the stairs, dear colleague. And I'll find my way better in the dark if I don't go down fast enough."

He passed round me and started swiftly down the stairs. I sighed and then joined Miss Aksentijević in the elevator. I expected her to push the ground floor button, but she just kept her finger on it. I looked at it questioningly.

"No one has to know that I went into Jelena's apartment," she said softly. "I will be very discreet. Just give me back my keys." She paused and a smile spread over her face. "I'm sure I can find a way to repay you for this service."

I reached inside my pocket and removed the set of keys. As she stretched out her hand to take them, I pulled out the latex gloves, put them on and then took the key I'd picked up from the floor of Miss Jakovljević's apartment out of my other pants pocket. Miss Aksentijević's hand fell again as she watched me compare the key to those on the key ring. It matched the third one I'd tried. I had some trouble taking it off because the ring was stiff. The latex on the tip of my forefinger and the nail underneath were torn in the process.

"I will pretend you haven't spoken," I said, putting the two identical keys into different pants pockets and removing the gloves. "I will return the key ring to you downstairs after I remove the key to the front door of the building."

Her narrowed eyes gave me a drop-dead stare and then she turned her head away. When it became clear that she did not intend to push the button, I did it myself. The lights in the corridor went out as the elevator doors were closing.

"Regardless of how discreet you tried to be, you would not escape Mr. Teodosijević's attention. And Adam's even less. I advise you not to try anything. You'll only get into trouble."

She did not reply and continued to look askance. We spent the rest of the ride down in silence. It was only when the doors opened at my back that I became aware of something strange. Being surrounded by mirrors had not made me ill at ease this time. No illusion had threatened reality.

"This is already worrisome, esteemed colleague," said Inspector Vesić who was waiting for us on the ground floor. "I understand why I reached the fifth floor by elevator faster than you did on foot, but why would I go down faster on foot than you did by elevator. . . .?"

"You never know what might slow you down."

"I hope you didn't run into ghosts again."

"This time it was something more innocuous. Isn't that right, Miss Aksentijević?"

She let out something that sounded like a snarl, then passed between the two of us and headed towards the exit. Opening the glass door briskly, she stepped outside and stood near it with her back turned. I preceded Inspector Vesić, held the door for him and then went out.

The wind had died down a little. There were not many whirlwinds of dust on the ground and the top of the linden was rustling more softly. Nevertheless, Miss Aksentijević drew the poncho around her, head bowed, as she stared at the tips of her shoes. She did not seem inclined to cooperate so I had to find the key to the front door by myself. After my second failed attempt, Inspector Vesić joined in.

"Allow me."

I thought he would keep on trying the keys, but all he did was lift up the set, shake it a little, causing it to jingle, then single one out.

"This is what you're looking for. Shall I take it off?"

I felt my torn nail. "Please do."

He placed his briefcase on the ground and took the keys in his cupped hands. For five or six seconds he seemed to be making a wad out of them, and when he opened his hands the set was in one hand and the key to the front door was in the other. Nothing was torn. I looked at them for a short time in disbelief, shaking my head, before taking them. He bowed with a smile. I did not have to check whether the key was the right one, of course. That would have been insulting. I put it in the pocket with the key I had removed and then handed the key ring to Miss Aksentijević.

"Here you are."

She almost yanked it out of my hand, but I had crooked my forefinger into the ring.

"I'll do my best to find Miss Jakovljević by Monday."

We stayed there joined by the key ring for several moments, eye to eye. Finally, I released the ring.

"Good night," she said coldly after throwing the keys in her briefcase. The hint of a smile softened her angry expression as she nodded to Inspector Vesić.

"Good night, Miss Aksentijević," he replied, removing his hat and bowing once more.

We watched in silence as she walked to the parking area, searched a while for the keys in the abyss of her briefcase, backed out a small red car and quickly drove off with a screech of tires.

"It's not easy with agents," said Inspector Vesić when the car's tail lights had disappeared at the end of the short street.

"Particularly not with literary agents." I paused. "Did you mean that seriously?"

"What?"

"About magic."

"Oh, that." He paused as well. "Unless it's a hoax, it must be magic."

"A hoax?"

"We're talking about the greatest challenge for all those who . . . have a special interest in locks. No one has yet managed to lock a door from the outside with a key that is located inside. Whoever succeeds will see their reputation soar. Unofficial reputation, of course, but no less desirable for that. So it's no wonder that people have resorted to various hoaxes."

"For example?"

"Usually there was another way out of the premises that were locked from the inside."

"There's no other way out of Miss Jakovljević's apartment. There are four windows but they are all closed."

"Maybe there's another exit that you didn't notice. You have to know what you're looking for in order to find it."

"But where could that secret exit lead? Certainly not into the apartment next door. That would already be a conspiracy. And who would hatch a complicated plot just to play a trick on a literary agent?"

"There's the roof too. No conspiracy would be needed if the exit led there."

I shook my head. "Some sort of hole would have to be visible on the ceiling, but I didn't notice any."

"Secret openings are the hardest to find."

"Even if I missed it, let's go back to the question of why. Who would go to the trouble of making a secret exit onto the roof just for the fun of it?"

"From what I understand, writers are rather eccentric."

"They are, for the most part. But not quite that much."

"Then all that's left is magic. I'd like to meet Miss Jakovljević when you find her. If she really did the impossible, she's worthy of my admiration."

"If I find her. . . ."

"You'll find her. Who else if not you? Writers are your specialty."

I smiled. "Thanks for your help, Inspector Vesić. I'm sorry to have bothered you this late."

"You did me a favor. The case could be quite interesting. I'd like to follow your progress."

"I'll keep you posted."

He pointed down the street.

"I'm parked nearby. There was no room here when I arrived. Good night, Inspector Lukić."

He put out his hand.

"Good night," I replied, shaking it.

Before I got into my car, I raised my eyes to the façade again. Only a few windows were still alight, but none of them was in the upper left-hand corner of the building.

〜 8 〜

I DIDN'T LEAVE RIGHT away. I put the gloves back on again and took Miss Jakovljević's telephone out of my pants pocket. I didn't have a spare pair, but there was just a little tear on the tip of the forefinger that I rarely use when handling a cellphone. I hit a button at random with my thumb and the screen turned on.

I went into the main menu and then messages received. But nothing was there. I stared at the screen in bewilderment until the blue glow faded. I went back to the menu and into the call register that recorded all the communications.

That screen was empty too, even though there should have been evidence of considerable activity. The agent, if no one else, had frequently called the writer on this telephone over the past two days. Even if someone had erased everything, no one could have removed the record of the last two calls. About an hour and a half ago Miss Aksentijević had let the chirping ring a long time to convince me that the cellphone was in the apartment. And then a little less than half an hour ago a message had arrived in my presence and then somehow disappeared, even though the telephone had been with me the whole time since then.

I kept my eyes on the screen even after it soon went dark again, until I finally figured out a possible explanation. The phone was set so it didn't record any calls, and messages were erased after they were read. This hadn't occurred to me right away because I never used this feature. Miss Jakovljević clearly had a reason not to allow anyone to trace her calls and messages if the cellphone were to fall into the wrong hands.

Luckily, evidence of this telephone's use was recorded in other places. I had reached for my cell to call the Communications Department at police headquarters, when I suddenly realized I didn't know Miss Jakovjlević's phone number. My first thought was to ask Miss Aksentijević, but I didn't take out her business card. Bearing in mind her mood when she'd left, I could hardly count on her obliging me.

Then it dawned on me that I didn't need her help. The number had to be somewhere on the phone's menu. I spent a good minute going through it, but finally gave up. Either the number wasn't there or I simply didn't know how to find it. If it was the former, then the owner of the phone had taken great pains to prevent any possible misuse.

I felt out of my depth and defeated, and then I realized there was a simple solution. I should have thought of it right away, but it seemed that fatigue had got the better of me. There was no need at all to search for the number. I would call my own phone with Miss Jakovljević's. Actually, it would be better to call the Communications Department directly. As, evidently, an extremely cautious person, the writer had probably turned off the identification of her number along with the other measures she'd taken. Nothing would appear on my screen. But she couldn't hide from the Department.

I looked at the contact list on my cell and punched the number of the Communications Department on the other phone with my thumb. After the fifth ring, I thought something strange was going on. Indeed, it was rather late, but the duty officer always answered promptly.

Someone finally picked up after the eighth ring, but didn't speak. Silence reigned for several moments.

"Hello?" came from the other end just as I was about to speak. The unfamiliar youngish male voice sounded surprised and cautious.

I must have hit the wrong number in the dark car, I concluded. Just in case, though, I asked, "Communications Department?"

This was followed by another brief silence.

"Yes," said the voice in the same tone.

"Hello, this is Inspector Dejan Lukić. I need some information about the phone I'm calling from."

The hesitation was repeated a third time.

"Where did you get that telephone, Inspector Lukić?"

Now it was my turn to pause slightly before answering.

"I was given a new case tonight. I found it in the apartment of the missing person. Why?"

For a moment I had the impression that the duty officer was talking to someone in a low voice. He cleared his throat before replying, ignoring my question.

"Could you come to the Communications Department right away? Don't use that telephone anymore."

I knew there was no point in repeating "Why?" I curbed my curiosity, replied, "I'm on my way," and ended the call.

As though Miss Jakovljević's telephone was breakable, I put it in the right inside pocket of my jacket. In my rush to get moving, I didn't take off the latex gloves.

∽ 9 ∾

THE COMMUNICATIONS DEPARTMENT WAS located on the top seventh floor of Police Headquarters. The display above the elevators indicated that both of them were up there. It seems something unusual is happening in Communications tonight, I thought as I waited for one of the elevators to reach the ground floor. As the doors closed behind me and the elevator started up, a feeling of slight discomfort set in. I had already reached the fourth floor when I realized what was causing it. I turned my back to the small mirror where my reflection gazed at me and the unease disappeared.

I expected to come across someone in the long corridor, but it was empty. There was no crowd in the central room of the Communications Department either. The middle of the large, round windowless room was filled with a massive curved control panel and row of monitors. Seen from the back, they looked like some sort of rampart. With the exception of a table lamp with a bell-like shade in one corner of the panel, there was no other light. The duty officer's face looked spectral in the grayish glow of the screens. Behind him by the opposite wall stood another man, but I couldn't get a good look at him in the gloom.

"Inspector Dejan Lukić," I said as I approached the control panel.

I thought I knew everyone who worked in the Communications Department, but I had never seen this man before. He couldn't have been more than twenty-five. His unkempt hair, stooped shoulders, hooded sweatshirt and conspicuous earring in his right ear were much more characteristic of a hacker, at least as I imagined them, than a police officer. I had never come here at this hour. The dress code seemed more relaxed on the night shift.

"Good evening, Inspector. Stanislav Mirić."

It was the voice I'd heard on Miss Jakovljević's telephone. He hadn't mentioned his title after his name, as was customary. I guessed he didn't think it necessary. Who else could he be but the Communications Department duty officer?

He got up from his office chair and extended his hand over the control panel. His long limbs made this an easy matter. It hadn't appeared so while he was sitting, probably because of his hunched posture, but he must have been a good six feet two. I was just about to shake his hand, when I became aware of the latex gloves. I quickly took off the right one, held it in my left hand and we shook hands.

"Sorry to ask you to come right away this late."

"There certainly must be a reason for it," I replied.

"I'd like to take a look at the phone you used to call me."

He stretched out his hand again, palm up. I put the glove I'd taken off into my right hand and with my left took Miss Jakovljević's cell out of my inside jacket pocket. But I didn't give it to him.

"There was no chance to check for fingerprints," I explained.

The young man nodded his head. He glanced around the control panel and found what he was looking for near the lamp. He had trouble putting the latex gloves on his large bony hands. As though they were not his size.

When he sat down again, his shoulders and head were visible above the rampart, but his hands were hidden. He did something briefly, looked up at me and then glanced behind him.

"Did you open the phone after we talked?"

"No, I didn't. I just put it in my pocket and drove over here. You told me not to use it."

Officer Mirić got up and headed for the wall behind the control panel. His tall frame completely concealed the man standing there. They spent about a minute whispering to each other. The young man shrugged his shoulders twice and once turned his head briefly toward me. Then he moved aside and a short, balding, corpulent man in his fifties stepped out of the shadows. His thumb and index finger were holding the top of a little transparent plastic bag containing Miss Jakovljević's cellphone.

"Our paths cross again, Inspector Lukić," he said.

I stared at him for several moments before replying.

"Good evening, Commissioner Milenković."

"It was good until you called the Communications Department. Which phone did you use?"

"Why, that one," I said in bewilderment, motioning to the little bag with my chin.

"Perhaps there's an error. Do you have any other?"

"Yes, my service phone."

"That's it?"

"That's it."

"You certainly must have a private cellphone."

"I certainly do, but I don't carry it with me when I'm on duty. It's at home. What's the problem, Commissioner?"

He ignored my question.

"Would you please let me see your service phone?"

I took it out of the left inside pocket of my jacket. The commissioner nodded to the young man, who went back to the control panel, took my cell and sat down again. As he was examining it, Commissioner Milenković came up to the control panel. He looked older in the subdued light. Or at any rate exhausted.

We spent about two minutes in silence. The commissioner first watched Officer Mirić as he worked and then raised his eyes to me. We stared at each other until the cellphone examination was over. The long-limbed officer raised his head toward his superior. Neither one spoke, nor did I notice them exchange signals. Nevertheless, the next moment my phone was given back to me.

It should have occurred to me earlier, I thought, reproaching myself. I had not met this young man before because he didn't work here. He was a member of Commissioner Milenković's team. But why had the National Security Agency taken over the Communications Department tonight?

"Where did you get this telephone?" asked the commissioner, raising the plastic bag a little.

"I already told Officer Mirić," I replied. "I'm on a new case. I took it from the apartment of the missing person."

"Who's the missing person?"

"Miss Jelena Jakovljević. She's a writer. Perhaps you've heard of her?"

The commissioner sighed instead of replying. "Literature again."

"It can't be helped, those are my kind of cases."

"We seem to share the same fate. Although literature's not my profession."

"Why would the National Security Agency be interested in a missing writer?"

"Because she has an unusual cellphone."

"Unusual?" I repeated after a short pause.

"Very. In particular, it doesn't leave any identification. And that can't happen here." He swept his outstretched finger over the monitors on the control panel. "But if it does happen, then it's a case for us."

"So, how's that possible?"

The commissioner shrugged his shoulders.

"It's possible. New things are being invented all the time in communications technology. If you don't keep an eye on developments, you fall behind before you know it and then you've got no protection whatsoever. But the lack of identification is the lesser of the two mysteries."

"What's the greater one?"

He eyed me silently for a moment before he spoke again.

"Are you quite certain that you didn't open the telephone after calling the Communications Department?" he asked in return.

"Quite. I had no reason to."

"Were you alone or with someone else?"

"Alone."

"I hope you're not hiding anything from me. Our cooperation was a bit flawed last time."

"I agree. It was rather one-way."

He seemed about to reply to this, but just looked at me again without speaking for several moments.

"If what you say is true, then the second mystery is really a whopper. There's no SIM card or battery in Miss Jakovljević's phone."

Now it was my turn to stare at him.

"But that's impossible," I said at last. "How . . . could I have talked to Officer Mirić?"

I hoped he hadn't noticed my hesitation. I decided at the last moment not to mention the message. The last time I'd worked with him had taught me not to reveal more than was necessary.

"Not even he knows how. And there's no one better in communications and information technology. Don't let appearances deceive you."

"I'll go through the phone with a fine tooth comb once again," interjected the young man, grinning awkwardly at the compliment. "But the SIM card and battery are definitely not where they should be and there's simply no other place for them." He rubbed his earring absentmindedly between his thumb and index finger. "I'll check the fingerprints too, if there are any."

"Of course," continued Commissioner Milenković, "great mysteries sometimes have simple, even commonplace solutions. Occam's razor. It might turn out that someone here is pulling our leg."

"Who would pull the National Security Agency's leg?"

He shook his head. "I don't know. Some joker. They crop up here and there."

"They would be a very stupid joker."

"I'm glad that you, as an intelligent man, realize that, Inspector Lukić. Well, let's leave the jokers alone for now. What did you find out about Miss Jakovljević?"

"Mostly what her agent Miss Aksentijević told me. She called the police tonight because she hadn't been able to contact the writer since Wednesday night. She was afraid that something had happened to her in her apartment. She couldn't go in and check because the door was locked from the inside."

"You broke into the apartment?"

"No, I didn't. There was no need. We have an expert who delicately opens any lock."

He knitted his brow.

"Vesić?"

"Vesić."

"He's got talent. Too bad he doesn't come and work for us. Did you find anyone in the apartment?"

"No."

"And it really was locked from the inside?"

"That's right."

"Was there any other way to get out?"

"If there was, I didn't notice it. All the windows were closed."

"Another mystery," he said in an even voice. "Did anything catch your eye in the apartment?"

"Nothing special. It was spic-and-span. Writers' apartments usually aren't like that."

"I had no idea."

"That's because you don't have much to do with literature."

"What little I have is quite enough. Please give me the address."

"Number 12 Oak Street. Apartment 19."

Although the young man had received no orders, he quickly typed the data on one of the keyboards.

"All right," said Commissioner Milenković. "That's all for now. Keep working on the case. If you track down the missing writer, I'd appreciate being informed without delay. I'd like to talk to her. Somewhere she got hold of a very interesting telephone."

"Cooperation goes without saying," I said flatly.

"I'm sorry I can't say I look forward to working with you again. Goodbye, Inspector Lukić."

"Good night."

I turned and headed for the door, but the commissioner's voice stopped me before I got there.

"Did you take anything else out of Miss Jakovljević's apartment?"

I turned around and shook my head.

"No, I didn't."

"So why did you take her cell, of all things?"

We stared fixedly at each other for a long moment. Finally I shrugged my shoulders.

"I thought it would be more useful with me than in an empty apartment. Now it isn't anymore."

The commissioner nodded his head slowly.

"Good night, Inspector."

～ 10 ～

I HAD JUST GOTTEN out of the elevator on the ground floor when my cellphone rang. As I took it out, I thought that it was Commissioner Milenković with a few more questions. But I saw on the screen that it was Inspector Prvoslav Bobić, the duty officer in my Investigations Department. As I'd entered the elevator on the seventh floor a few moments ago, I had briefly considered going down to my office on the fifth floor. One look at the clock had made me change my mind. My shift had ended at midnight, four minutes ago, and I had no other business to take care of there.

"Hello," I said.

"Mr. Branislav Teodosijević would like to speak with you. He says it's urgent."

"Please transfer the call to my office. I'm on the ground floor. I'll be up shortly."

"All right."

I re-entered the elevator, as the doors hadn't closed. I heard the telephone ringing in my office as soon as I stepped onto the fifth floor. It sounded piercing in the quiet corridor with its subdued lights.

I picked up the receiver without turning the light on. "Inspector Dejan Lukić."

"I'm sorry to disturb you so late, Inspector. But I thought you might be interested. There's someone in Miss Jakovljević's apartment."

I wanted to ask three or four questions all at once, but had enough presence of mind to refrain. They would keep.

"I'm on my way," I replied.

Driving quickly to Oak Street, I concluded that I had probably achieved nothing by not talking to Mr. Teodosijević on my cell. I had started working with Commissioner Milenković again, which meant that they were checking all my telephones. And probably my movements. Even if Officer Mirić was not the wizard his superior made him out to be, he could have planted some monitoring device in the short time he was supposedly checking out my cellphone. Indeed, they must have realized I hadn't overlooked this. They couldn't have underestimated me. We had played this game before. . . .

As soon as I got out of the car in the parking area, I looked up at the façade of the building at number 12. Only three windows were still lit up and they were all quite far from the upper left-hand corner. I hastened toward the entrance, unlocked the door and entered the building. I didn't push the light switch in the foyer and headed for the elevator in the gloom.

The elevator was on the fourth floor. I pushed the call button and as it slowly descended I realized that I actually should have taken the stairs. If someone had really gone into Miss Jakovljević's apartment, they might not have left the building. I would miss them if they went down the stairs just as I was going up in the elevator. In the stairwell, though, I would have heard the elevator.

Although there was no need, I waited for the elevator

to reach the ground floor. The doors opened, revealing the empty interior lined with mirrors. I hurried back to the foyer, turned on the lights and then ran up the stairs. I tried to be as quiet as possible, my ears pricked, but there was no humming of the elevator. Nothing disturbed the building's nocturnal peace.

As I reached the fifth floor, my panting broke the silence. I was already heading down the corridor when, just like last time, I stopped in mid-step and turned towards the stairs. My internal counter seemed to be seriously out of whack. Now there were only sixty-nine stairs. At some point I would have to go up—or even better, go down—when I wasn't agitated and taking two or three steps at a time. Just to see if I could count them correctly.

I paused briefly at the end of the corridor, my breathing subdued. Although it was just my imagination, I could almost feel Mr. Teodosijević and Adam standing behind the right-hand door. When I turned towards the door on the left, I had the impression that a silent void was gaping behind it. I went up and pressed my ear to the wooden surface.

I stayed that way against the door but didn't hear anything. Finally I stepped back and took out Miss Aksentijević's key. Had I needed latex gloves again I would have been in a fix. I'd taken off the other one as soon as I'd left the central room in the Communications Department and thrown both into a waste basket in the corridor, considering that I wouldn't need them anymore that night.

As I took the elevator back down to the ground floor of Police Headquarters after talking to Mr. Teodosijević, it had dawned on me that I might need them. I briefly considered going back to my office for a new pair of gloves, but then I would have lost several possibly vital minutes.

I inserted the key in the lock, turned it twice, pulled

it out and put it back in my pocket. I did all of this very quietly, at least as far as my ears were concerned. The lights went out just as I pulled down on the handle.

I didn't open the door right away, wondering whether I should first turn on the lights in the corridor again. No, it was better not to be seen. If someone was still inside, there in the dark they would have an advantage over me if I was in the light. I waited briefly for my eyes to adjust to the darkness, then opened the door just wide enough to slip inside.

I paused as soon as I had stepped inside the apartment and stood stock-still for several moments, listening. As there was no sound or movement, I groped for the handle behind my back and slowly closed the door. Everything was still. Finally I pushed the light switch. The radiance that filled the hallway, pouring out of the rectangular ceiling light, forced me to squint.

I stopped in front of the door leading to the larger room. It was ajar at the same angle as when I'd left there a little over an hour ago. I opened it slowly to my right until it reached the shelf. Behind it was a triangular space, large enough to hold a slender person. I entered the room and returned the door to its original position. There was no one behind it.

I didn't have to turn on the light to determine that the rest of the room was also empty. I entered the smaller room as far as the sliding door that led to the kitchen. I peered left and right through the upper part of the door and then turned on the light, pushed the door aside and entered. I went up to the closet and opened it. No one was hiding there either. I had suspected such an outcome, but verification takes precedence over suspicions in an investigator's job. Nevertheless, there are limits. I didn't check the refrigerator.

I closed the closet, pulled the sliding door shut and turned off the light. As I headed toward the bathroom, I figured that if I were to discover no one, there were only two possibilities left. Either Mr. Teodosijević was mistaken or whoever had been in Miss Jakovljević's apartment had left before I got there.

I waited two or three seconds for the neon light to go on before opening the bathroom door. The whiteness of the empty room blinded me again. Everything was just as I had left it. I was about to close the door when my duty to verify made me stop. I went over to the bathtub, grabbed the left edge of the plastic curtain and pulled. The yellow ducky was just where I'd left it.

I studied it briefly and then pulled the curtain closed. I exited the bathroom, shut the door and turned off both lights. As I stood in the darkness only slightly softened by the streetlight outlining the window, I thought with a sigh that I had come back in vain. My hand was already heading for the knob on the front door, when a sharp "ping" came from behind me.

Shivers began crawling down the back of my head and neck. I quickly turned toward the large room from where the noise had come, but all I could see was the upper contour of the desk. I shook my head, angry at myself. Of course, I should have turned on the light when I went into the main room a moment ago. Then I probably would not have overlooked what was on the desk, even if it was small. But I had been looking for something larger that could be seen in the gloom. . . .

I stopped at the door and hit the switch. Even though I knew what I would see, I stared nonetheless in disbelief at the small black object next to the keyboard. The last time I'd seen it was about half an hour ago in Commissioner Milenković's little bag. How had it got back here?

As I walked toward the desk, I realized that this was the wrong question. There might be cellphones that don't leave any identification in the Communications Department and even work without a SIM card and battery, but they certainly aren't magical. This could not be the same telephone that I had taken with me. Someone had indeed been in the apartment after my departure and had left an identical cellphone in the same spot where I'd found the first. And now they had sent a new message on it.

I reached for the little device, but stayed my hand. I needed those latex gloves after all. Well, since I don't have them, I'll have to make do without, I thought. I reached into my pocket for my handkerchief, but then concluded that the precaution was unnecessary. I didn't have to take account of the fingerprints. Officer Mirić would look for them on the first telephone. I suspected, however, that his efforts would be in vain. Whoever was behind this seemed to me cautious enough not to allow such a commonplace mistake.

I picked up the cellphone. Even though I knew it had to be just an illusion, I couldn't get rid of the impression that there was something special about the way the smooth metal back of the phone touched my palm. I hadn't felt that with the previous phone, as though the thin latex of the gloves had insulated me from the unusual effect, if it had been there too.

I remembered which button to push. The New Message notification disappeared, the blue turned white and the same two words came up just like the last time.

"Find me."

I stared at them, deep in thought, until they disappeared. This was indisputably meant for me. One message could accidentally arrive when I was leaving Miss Jakovljević's apartment, but two such incidents within a short time ruled out any coincidence. Someone was determined to play tricks on me and I had no idea who, why or how.

I saw only one way to try and find out. My thumb hovered above the little buttons once again, but I didn't touch any of them. I would answer the message a little later. In another place, not here. And when I didn't have my service cellphone with me. In any case, I was in no hurry. Let whoever wanted to play stew in their own juices for a while, if they expected me to reply right away.

I put the phone in the right inside pocket of my jacket and headed out of the apartment.

∽ 11 ∾

I FELT FOR THE lock in the dark corridor, locked the door and turned around. I could not even make out the entrance to the apartment across the way. I thought of feeling along the wall to find the doorbell too, but concluded that it would be better to turn on the lights. Otherwise I would have trouble seeing where to enter Mr. Teodosijević's apartment. I stretched out my hand and walked toward where I thought the switch should be, but a light flashed on before I touched the opposite wall.

"You'll have no trouble seeing without that, Inspector Lukić," said the tall man in a black robe. He was standing at the open door with bright illumination behind him. Adam was by his left foot. The dog just looked at me inquisitively, making no sound.

"I thought you didn't turn the lights on in your apartment," I said as though justifying myself.

"There's no reason to when we are alone. But we must make allowances for the special needs of our visitors."

"Sight might even turn out to be a drawback," I said, hoping he could tell by the tone of my voice that I was smiling.

"It's certainly not an advantage in the dark." He returned my smile more with his lips than his tone. "Please come in."

He moved aside and motioned for me to enter. Adam also retreated from the entrance.

As soon as I entered, I realized that the apartment

was identical to the one I had just left. Actually, its mirror image. The bathroom here was on the right and the large room was on the left. The small room in front of me contained a square table with one chair. Piles of books were stacked on the table and the empty wall behind it framed the window.

Mr. Teodosijević closed the door. Moving with confident steps, he circumvented me and entered the large room. Adam went into the smaller room and joined him from that direction.

"Please come in," he repeated.

I stopped at the entrance to the room and looked around. What I saw was quite different from Miss Jakovljević's apartment. Indeed, the walls here were also completely covered, but not with bookshelves. The large room resembled an art gallery closely hung with paintings. Although they were of different sizes, their thin frames fit together nicely, creating a mosaic without any unused space. The effect was harmonious, almost like wallpaper, because the white canvases contained only red and black brush strokes, and the rectangles were separated by rust-colored wooden borders.

In the middle of the room under a blazing ceiling light stood an easel. The tall round stool in front of it had a palette and two brushes on the seat. A dark-blue cloth had been placed over the large canvas on the easel. The entire floor was lined with newspaper spattered here and there with paint, particularly around the easel.

There was almost no furniture. A narrow cot extended under the two windows and a plaid blanket had been thrown over the unmade sheets. On the opposite side of the room, centered against the wall, was a worn and cracked brown leather armchair.

"Take a seat," said Mr. Teodosijević, indicating the armchair. Then he approached the bed, grabbed hold of the metal frame and sat down. Adam followed him and dropped to the floor by his side.

"I won't keep you," I said. "It's late."

"Not for me. I do most of my work at night." His lips curved into a smile again. "That's the privilege of a painter who doesn't depend on daylight." This time his tone of voice was fitting. "Please," he added, motioning to the armchair once more.

As I sank into it, the springs creakingly complained. I waited for him to speak first, but he remained silent. I had the uncomfortable feeling that blind eyes were examining me.

"There is no one in Miss Jakovljević's apartment," I said, breaking the silence.

"I know. You were too late," he said with a tinge of reproach. "They left just before you got here."

"You didn't do anything this time." I hoped he had not missed the reciprocated reproach in my voice.

"Because I would not have had the advantage of the dark. Whoever was in Miss Jakovljević's place did not turn on the lights in the corridor."

"Perhaps they had a flashlight."

"Perhaps. But maybe they didn't need one."

"Why do you think so?"

"This was no amateur burglar who would be bothered by the dark. Everything was done quite skillfully. And silently."

"But you heard them nonetheless. How else would you know that they'd entered the apartment next door?"

"I wasn't the one who heard them. Although my hearing is very keen, I would have missed them. But not Adam."

He lowered his hand unerringly to the dog's head and patted it lightly.

"Perhaps Adam made a mistake."

The corners of his mouth turned up briefly.

"Adam never makes mistakes."

"We all make mistakes sometimes. For example, you

claimed that Miss Jakovljević was in the apartment and there's no one there."

The green jade seemed to flash for a moment.

"Jelena did not come out of there," he said softly.

"In any case, we have a new mystery before us. Why did a professional break into Miss Jakovljević's apartment? There are no signs of a break-in. Everything is just the same as the first time I went inside."

"Of course there's no sign of a break-in. What the burglar was looking for did not require a search or any unnecessary noise."

"How do you know what the burglar was looking for?"

His expression turned sneering.

"You don't have to be particularly insightful, Inspector, to figure that out. There's only one thing of value in the apartment across the way that would warrant a burglary."

I eyed him dubiously.

"I found nothing there more valuable than books. Indeed, I didn't have a chance to examine them in detail. Is there an old and expensive edition on the shelves?"

"Expensive yes, but it's not old and it's not on the shelves."

"Are there expensive new editions?"

"Yes, if there's only one copy."

"I didn't know that books were printed in only one copy."

"This one isn't printed. That's why it's not on the shelves."

"How can it be a book if it isn't printed?"

"I didn't say it was a book. It's a manuscript. Actually, a computer file. Miss Jakovljević's new novel. *Find Me.*"

I scrutinized him again briefly in silence.

"I thought that only Miss Aksentijević considered

the manuscript valuable. Why would a burglar be interested in it?"

"Miss Aksentijević is certainly not the only one trying to get hold of it. Might I ask—what did she tell you, why does she need it?"

"She has to submit it to the publisher on Monday. And she is personally quite keen to do so, even though she's only her agent."

"Double agent."

"Double literary agent?"

"That's right. Miss Jakovljević caught on to her double game. That's why she was avoiding her. Miss Aksentijević would have submitted the manuscript, indeed, but certainly not to the publisher."

"To whom else?"

"To the highest bidder. A lot of people are after it."

"A lot of people?"

"You can't imagine how many want to read it, particularly if it's finished."

"Miss Jakovljević must write really exciting novels if her readers don't have the patience to wait for the book and break into her computer to get hold of the manuscript. She would be the envy of every writer."

Mr. Teodosijević stroked Adam before he replied.

"These are not ordinary readers."

"Burglar-readers certainly aren't ordinary."

"That's not what makes them exceptional."

"So what does?"

"They'd give anything to be the first to read the manuscript."

"I don't understand. Why do they care so much about being the first?"

He did not reply immediately. When he spoke, his voice was hushed.

"Because this might be the Grand Manuscript."

"Grand Manuscript?" I repeated.

"Haven't you heard about it?"

I shook my head. A moment later I realized that this was not enough and hastened to say, "No, I haven't."

"Those awaiting its advent believe that the first reader will become immortal."

We sank into silence. I knew I should say something, but nothing appropriate came to mind.

"No less," I said finally.

"Although this must seem like pure superstition to a police inspector, I don't recommend that you underestimate the adherents of the Grand Manuscript. These people will do anything to reach their goal."

"It's no wonder, if they really believe the reward is immortality. But immortality is usually connected to serious literature, not detective novels."

"Literary quality is not decisive in this regard."

"I see you are well-informed about the Grand Manuscript's state of affairs."

"Only so-so. All I know is what Miss Jakovljević told me."

"So that means she knew she was writing the Grand Manuscript?"

"She knew that something strange had been happening ever since she started working on the novel *Find Me*. Odd characters kept importuning her with bewildering bids and unbelievable stories about the Grand Manuscript. She didn't take them seriously at first, but as her writing progressed they became increasingly insistent. That's why she had to withdraw completely from the public eye."

"She did a splendid job. But now that it's all over, she can resurface."

"All over?"

"Well, if the burglar got hold of the new novel's manuscript from her computer, then no one will harass her anymore. All that's left is to see which lucky person becomes immortal after reading it first."

"The burglar left empty-handed, of course. Don't

forget that Miss Jakovljević writes detective novels. A computer is the last place she would leave a manuscript she wanted to hide."

"Then it's strange that the burglar didn't look for it somewhere else. If they did, they left no traces."

"Of course not. This was not an ordinary burglar. Nevertheless, I doubt that they found anything."

"Miss Jakovljević is the only one who could tell us that. And we don't know where she is."

"She did not leave her apartment," repeated Mr. Teodosijević like a mantra, after a brief hesitation.

I didn't know what to say to this. The armchair creaked beneath me again as I got up. On the other side of the room, the man and his dog rose in concert that same moment.

"It's time for me to go," I said. "There's nothing more I can do here and I have to get up early in the morning. I'm on duty over the weekend."

I was already at the door to the small hall when something crossed my mind.

"Those pictures of yours in Miss Jakovljević's apartment are interesting. Those are her eight books, right?"

He nodded his head and gestured broadly towards the walls.

"Those are all books. That is my library."

∽ 12 ∽

I CLIMBED INTO BED and then took the cellphone from the bedside table where its ebony color seemed to absorb the glow of the green-shaded table lamp. When I had it in the palm of my hand, once again I seemed to feel an eerie prickle.

The precautionary measures I'd taken now seemed excessive. It's easy, however, to fall prey to paranoia when the National Security Agency complicates your life. I left my service cellphone in the kitchen all the way on the other side of the living room. If it was set to serve as a microphone, it would have a hard time picking up anything through two doors.

And what was there to pick up, anyway? My bedroom is quiet at night, particularly when I'm alone. I don't snore, as far as I know. At least none of the ladies who have spent the night with me there have ever complained about it. Indeed, they may have avoided mentioning the little nocturnal annoyance out of consideration. . . .

The telephone had a camera too, although I doubted that even a real wizard could have set it in less than a minute to send pictures. But just in case, I'd covered the phone with a cloth.

In fact, the simplest course would have been to remove the battery. Then there would be no way to misuse the device. But I didn't. Disabling it would only indicate that I was on to them and intended to do something I didn't want them to see. This way, everything would appear normal.

There could be other cameras though. What if someone had been here after my run-in with Commissioner Milenković and now they could watch a live broadcast from my apartment? I winced at the possibility. After giving it some thought, I concluded nevertheless that this was going too far. Even the National Security Agency would have to get a court order for something like that and it would take quite a while to do so during the night.

No authorization would be needed, however, if they placed the camera somewhere outside my apartment. For example, in the foliage of the oak tree next to my bedroom window. I'd drawn the drapes before going to bed, something I rarely do because it makes me feel confined. But they didn't know that. If they really intended to spy on me through the window, it would be natural for them to assume I pulled the drapes every night, not just because I wanted to thwart them.

It was not until I lay there staring at the little black cellphone in my hand that I realized I'd given paranoia free rein and feared those who might not be threatening me at all, while disregarding the real danger. Suddenly I felt stripped bare before the mysterious telephone that seemed to return my gaze from the dark screen, penetrating deep inside me.

Wanting to chase away this uncomfortable feeling, I raised my thumb to call up the message. All at once I was struck by the realization that I should not have postponed my reply. If the second cell was the same as the first, the message had been erased after I'd read it and the number would be impossible to find.

I wouldn't hesitate to disturb Miss Aksentijević in the dead of night, regardless of how she felt about me, but it had just become clear that this would be pointless. The number she had given me would certainly not belong to either this telephone or the other one that was now with Commissioner Milenković. There must be a third cellphone in the writer's apartment—an ordinary one with a SIM card and battery. I hadn't found it because I hadn't looked for it after taking the first one, considering it to be all there was.

The thought about the SIM card led me to turn the telephone over in my hand. I fumbled a bit until I discovered how to open the cover, then raised it and saw what I had expected. The place for the SIM card was empty. Soon my other suspicion was also confirmed. There wasn't any battery. I replaced the cover, turned the phone over again and stared in frustration at the front of it for several moments.

As I was about to put it back on the bedside table, I thought, why not give it a try? One should never take anything for granted about a device that stumped even the National Security Agency. My thumb danced about the buttons. I sighed in relief when Messages showed one was there. I pushed another button and two words appeared once again on a white background: *"Find me."*

I gazed at them for a while, uncertain what to reply. A multitude of ideas swarmed in my head, jockeying for precedence. In the end I decided to start with the basics. Although it appeared obvious, I had to establish who had sent the message.

"Miss Jakovljević?" I typed.

Even though the cellphone had neither a SIM card nor a battery, confirmation appeared on the screen that the message had been sent. I did not fear that sending this message would let the National Security Agency know I had another unusual telephone. They already knew I had it. If they'd wanted to take it away from me, they would have done so immediately after the last time it had been used—when the message appeared on it while I was in Miss Jakovljević's apartment the second time. They would most likely have come for it themselves instead of asking me again to take it to them.

But they hadn't done anything, which could only mean that they'd decided to let me use it so they could monitor me through it. Very well, I would keep that in mind. Then it dawned on me that there was another possibility, although highly improbable. What if even the National Security Agency couldn't see when this phone was used?

There was no time to dwell on this matter because a "ping" rang out. It sounded thunderous in the quiet of the night. It might even have reached the kitchen. I hastened to open the message.

"Good evening, Inspector Lukić. How are you?"

I smiled and quickly replied:

"Fine, thanks. How are you?"

As soon as I had pushed the Send button, I searched through the menu to turn down the volume. Before I could figure out how to do it, there was another "ping". I stopped what I was doing to open the new message.

"Wonderful."

I didn't reply immediately and continued to examine the menu, fearing it might not be possible to adjust the volume. That would be troublesome. Luckily, however, it could be done. Instead of turning it down, I switched it off and turned on the vibration.

"That's nice to hear. So this means we can close the case."

Moments later, the little device trembled in my hand. She was clearly more skillful than I at texting.

"Does it seem over to you?"

"The police case, yes. Someone is reported missing. They are found. In good shape, by their own statement. The investigation is called off."

"Has everything really been resolved?"

"What hasn't been resolved is not within police jurisdiction. No one has broken the law."

"There are some peculiarities, though. Will the police turn a blind eye to them?"

"The police are not interested in a writer's private life, regardless of how peculiar it is."

"And you personally?"

"Me?"

"You have a degree in literature, don't you?"

"You are well-informed."

"It comes in handy. One would expect you to be interested in a writer's private life. Unless your studies left you with a bad opinion of detective novels and you carry prejudices against their authors. . . ."

"My studies taught me that every prejudice in literature is wrong. And that the main division is into good novels and bad novels. Regardless of whether they are detective stories or any other."

"If this were a detective story, it would be wrong to end it here. Many questions would go unanswered."

"But it's not a detective story and reality is under no obligation to provide a satisfactory ending."

"Who knows what obligations reality has? Let's not go into that now. So you're giving up?"

"As I said, there is no reason to continue with the investigation now that you have told me you are fine."

"A police inspector should not be so credulous. What proof do you have?"

I felt this was a trap, but there was no retreating.

"Your statement. These messages."

"You would use messages exchanged with a telephone that has no SIM card or battery?"

Before I could think of an answer, a new question arrived.

"Even if you use them, are you sure they will still be there when you need them?"

Of course I wasn't sure, but I was spared the embarrassment of having to admit it by the fourth question that soon followed.

"Finally, even if the messages are saved, do they prove that you were actually in contact with Jelena Jakovlje-vić?"

"Aren't I?" I answered at last.

"Maybe you are and maybe you aren't. That remains for you to establish beyond reasonable doubt. As you see, the case is still open. You still haven't found the missing person. We are far from a satisfactory ending."

"Like in a detective novel?"

"Like in a detective novel. Good night, Inspector Lukić. Sweet dreams."

∽ 13 ∾

THE DOORS STARTED TO close as soon as I stepped inside the elevator. That was strange. I hadn't pressed any button. I looked to my left where the panel of buttons was located but there was nothing there. I thought I must be mistaken and it was on the right. But nothing troubled the glass surface there either.

I turned in bewilderment toward the doors just as the two sides touched and joined the halves of my face together. Staring into my own wide eyes, I felt trapped. Even though I was not claustrophobic, an unbearable feeling of confinement swept over me. I had to get out of the elevator as soon as possible.

I did the only thing that crossed my panic-stricken mind—I tried to dig my nails into the barely visible gap between the two doors to separate them. A moment later, however, I jumped away from the doors; the elevator had started and it was moving in an impossible direction. Even though I was on the top floor, the elevator began to ascend. I could clearly tell that I was going up—and much faster than the elevator's usual speed.

Feeling unsteady, I looked reflexively for something to hold on to, but all I could do was place my hands on the smooth wall in front of me. Instead of anchoring me, however, staring at my equally unsteady reflection only increased my instability.

As I took my hands off the glass, I had the impression that the reflected hands would not let go of me. With a yank, I backed away to the middle of the little compartment. I no longer dared to go near any of the walls. I had the impression that my replicas from all sides, even from above, were reaching out to me for support.

Not from all sides, however. There was no threat from the red carpeting under my feet. The thick weave did not reflect anything. I quickly squatted, placed my fists on the floor and bowed my head, looking between my shoes. This position made it easier to bear the elevator's rapid speed as it continued inexplicably upwards.

The change began as I was feverishly trying to figure a way out of my predicament. Even though I could still feel the rough texture of the carpeting under my clenched fingers, what I saw clashed with it. The red changed to light blue, then lost its solidity and quickly dissolved. If I dared believe my own eyes, I was squatting on the gently rippling surface of the water.

A new panic attack was blocked by my sense of touch that still informed me I had a solid floor beneath me and there was no risk of sinking. But something was rising slowly from the depths. Even before it reached the surface, I detected an enormous human face. Not until it was directly beneath the soles of my shoes did I finally recognize it. Constructed solely of water, it appeared diffuse and unstable.

Miss Aksentijević started to say something, but nothing could be heard. Then her distorted voice reached my ears as though muffled.

". . . .Because Jelena has recently started to lose faith in what she writes, even though it has made her famous. And rich. It's as though she's had enough of detective novels. . . ."

The mouth kept moving but the voice fell silent as the face began to sink. As it sank, the color of the floor beneath me started to change again. At first I thought the water would turn back into carpeting. The blue changed to red, not a darker shade but the red of a brightly flaming fire.

Considerable willpower was needed to regain confidence in my sense of touch and not jump away from the fire that was raging on the elevator floor. The absence of heat was also inconsistent with the roaring flames. Quite the contrary, I started to shiver as though engulfed in cold air.

The fiery tongues were at first chaotic and then started to entwine, creating a form. Sculpting in fire was no easy matter. Just as the facial features stabilized, they melted away. Finally, they settled long enough for the teashop proprietor to speak in a crackling voice.

". . . .There you have three musicians, two painters, a sculptor and a writer. . . ."

As soon as this was said, the face deconstructed and the fire quickly subsided. The flames dwindled and went out. Several glowing spots lasted a little longer before they too disappeared. Finally all that remained was pitch blackness.

The new change in color was the most subtle. I barely noticed that the darkness had grown slightly paler. I had to strain to make out the rectangular hole gaping in the floor.

The clay packed hard in the bottom suddenly became loose and swollen as though something was trying to emerge. First a forehead was formed, then eyes, cheeks, a chin. It was not until the mouth appeared that I recognized the earthen face of Inspector Vesić. The mouth opened but no sound was heard until lumps stopped falling inside it.

"You have to know what you're looking for in order to find it," said my colleague.

His cheerful tone seemed to induce the next change in the elevator floor. The dark grave quickly dissolved and welled blue, no longer the turquoise of the deep sea but the diaphanous hue of a sunny sky.

Several scattered clouds were the only blemish on the overall brightness. As though set in motion by an imperceptible wind, they started to gather and lose their amorphousness. When the downy montage was composed, I recognized the face now being shown to me by the two cloudless jade spaces in place of the eyes.

The swollen lips of white diaphanous matter uttered a divine proclamation in a slow, deep voice.

"Those awaiting its advent believe that the first reader will become immortal."

Mr. Teodosijević's words still filled my ears as the montage broke up. The clouds did not scatter but dispersed, leaving no trace behind them. Nothing disturbed the blue anymore.

The splendor of the day did not last long, however. The square frame of the floor filled first with crimson and then darkness. This time pitch blackness was honeycombed with a multitude of twinkling points. Although it was quite obvious, the realization took a while to reach my consciousness. I was squatting on stars.

This seemed rather unbecoming, so I stood up hastily. In the process, I realized that the elevator was not moving. It was no longer going up. In all the commotion I had failed to notice when it stopped.

I wondered in bewilderment where it had reached and my eyes, still looking downward, provided the answer. This would surely have alarmed me were it not for the much greater fear that swept over me that same moment.

Despite all the floor's changes, it had been my sole support since entering the elevator. Now it had magically disappeared and I started falling out into the cosmic void. My hands flailed about, trying to hold on to something, but my fingers only slid down the smooth surface of the mirrors. I opened my mouth to scream, but no sound arose in airless space.

∽ 14 ∾

MY PANIC INTENSIFIED WHEN the stars suddenly went out. I stared wide-eyed at the impenetrable darkness around me. Several terrifying moments passed before it slowly dawned on me. I couldn't scream, but I was still breathing, actually panting with excitement. And there would be no breathing out in space. . . .

Even without light, I finally figured out where I was: sitting in bed. I'd just snapped awake from a nightmare. I was surrounded by darkness because I'd drawn the drapes. I shook my head to scatter the last remnants of the dream before placing my feet on the floor. I felt for my slippers, put them on, got up and headed for the window, arms outstretched.

When I pulled the drapes open, I was dazzled by the sun. I closed my eyes reflexively and turned my head. When I reopened my eyes, a bright white circle still flickered before them for a while. I'd been certain for some reason that the sun wasn't up, yet here the morning was well under way. The agitation that had subsided now returned. I'll be late for work.

As I rushed back to the bed and grabbed the cellphone from the bedside table to see what time it was, I remembered that my service phone was in the kitchen. It made no difference, this one probably had a clock too. It vibrated the moment I picked it up.

I glanced at the four numbers in the corner—08:14—before opening the new message.

Didn't sleep well? We overslept too. . . .

I pushed the button angrily to remove the message from the screen. I had left my innocent cell in the kitchen just because it had spent a few moments in the hands of one of Commissioner Milenković's men and had left this mysterious device in the bedroom that could do who knows what. Take pictures in the dark, let's say. Otherwise, why the allusion to my not sleeping well?

There was no time to go into that now. I looked around, trying to find a place to put the black telephone while I got dressed. I stuck it under the pillow and then hurried into the bathroom. I'm no fan of reality shows and would be quite unhappy to take part in one. . . .

At 08:42 I was ready to leave. I hesitated briefly about which cell to take. It seemed safest to take only my private phone, but I couldn't do without my service phone at work. In the end I decided to take all three. I put my private and service phones in the inside pockets of my jacket. The telephone from Miss Jakovljević's apartment vibrated so softly that it would be inconspicuous in my pants pocket.

Traffic is light on Saturday, so I quickly advanced toward police headquarters. I was not far away when the phone in my left jacket pocket started to ring. I don't like to talk on a cell while driving, but now I was in a hurry. Holding the steering wheel with one hand, I took out my service phone and saw the name of Inspector Ognjen Prokopović on the screen. I was on duty with him today.

"I'll be up in three minutes," I said without preliminaries.

"Maybe you won't, Inspector Lukić. A break-in was reported at 12 Oak Street. I thought you'd be interested. I see in the record that you were there last night."

"Yes, I was. Which apartment was broken into?"

"Let me see . . . number 19. An on-site investigation team has already been sent."

"I'll go there right away."

I was already well on my way to Oak Street when I realized there was no reason to rush, so I slowed down. It made no difference if I got there sooner or later. The police were already on the site, so the damage could not be any greater than it already was.

A patrol car was parked in front of the entrance. I left my car in one of the two available spots. As I got out of the car, I looked once again at the upper left-hand corner of the five-story building. All the windows were still closed. As I drew near to the building, I recognized the heavy, mustachioed policeman standing in the foyer where Miss Aksentijević had been waiting for me the night before. He wasn't at all bothered by the wind, particularly since it had died down considerably during the night. He'd probably gone inside so as not to appear unnecessarily conspicuous.

"Good morning, Inspector," he muttered, opening the door for me.

"Good morning, Vranešević."

"Fifth floor."

"I know."

"Inspectors Kostić and Zarić are up there."

I nodded and continued on to the elevator, then called it. Just as it started down from the top floor, my dream came vividly to mind. If I'd been alone in the foyer, I would have taken the stairs. Since there was no reason to hurry, I could finally count them carefully. But if I avoided the elevator, Vranešević's suspicions would be aroused. I didn't have to explain anything to him, of course, but rumors about me would soon start to spread. Policemen are much more inclined to gossip than people think. And not much is needed to get them started.

I looked down at the floor as soon as I got inside and pushed the button. As the doors met behind me, I waited in dread for the elevator to shoot upward. I felt no relief, however, when this failed to happen, since the ascent took the opposite extreme. The elevator seemed to climb considerably more slowly than before. After some time, the ride should already have been over, but it seemed never to end. I wanted to check our progress on the display, but was afraid of confronting my reflections in the mirrors. Finally, just as I was starting to get jumpy, the elevator stopped. I exited backwards without waiting for the doors to open all the way.

In front of Miss Jakovljević's apartment stood Inspector Zarić and a middle-aged woman in dark-blue overalls, a kerchief tied around her head. The tall, lean, balding inspector was holding a notepad and pencil. Next to the cleaning lady was a red plastic bucket with a long handle of the same color sticking out, its tip leaning against the wall.

"Hello, Inspector Lukić," said Zarić when I reached them. "This is Mrs. Sokolović. She's been working here for 17 years. She's the one who reported the break-in. Inspector Kostić is inside, taking pictures." He shook his head. "I've never seen such a . . . mess."

"The door was ajar. All I did was peek inside," said the cleaner, as though defending herself. "Poor Miss Jakovljević. Everything's ruined. It's awful. . . ." She stopped for a moment. "I didn't touch anything. I called you right away."

She patted the large pocket of her overalls, showing the contours of a cellphone.

"You did the right thing," I replied with a smile. "We won't keep you once you have made a statement. Please don't clean on the fifth floor anymore today."

She nodded quickly. Obviously she could barely wait to get out of there.

I raised my elbow to push the door all the way open, but before doing so I turned to Mrs. Sokolović.

"Did you see anyone in the corridor?"

Zarić answered for her. "No, she didn't. I asked." He tapped on his notebook with the end of his pencil.

"Not a soul," she replied hastily. "I rarely run into anyone on Saturday. People sleep in."

Now I nodded, with another smile.

Even before I entered Miss Jakovljević's apartment, I could tell from the entrance what awaited me inside. When the door opened, before me lay the exact opposite of the excessive tidiness I'd found the night before. Inspector Zarić's hesitant description of it as a "mess" was a gross understatement.

There was not a single book on the shelves next to the window at the end of the small room. They had been thrown onto the round glass table, the chairs and the floor. I entered the short hall and looked with foreboding through the right-hand door into the large room. Burglars leave a variety of scenes behind them. With some there is not the slightest trace, as though they haven't been there at all. Others, on the contrary, seem to take great pains to cause as much damage as possible, either from the frustration of leaving without the expected booty or just as a prank. This, however, looked like the work of a psychopath who really hated books for some reason.

Had I not been a book lover, I wouldn't have been so affected by what I saw. As a policeman I'd come across considerably worse sights, but as a professional I had not let them affect me personally. The emptied shelves here seemed eerie and when I lowered my eyes to the literally hundreds of books scattered about the three-seater, desk and floor, something tightened in my chest. The square rug that covered the center of the room was barely visible beneath the pile of books.

I heard footsteps in the small room. Inspector Kostić appeared in the opening that connected it to the large room, holding a camera. He was short and stout, with a thick red beard and round wire-rimmed glasses.

"Hello, Inspector. What do you have to say about this jumble?"

I shook my head. "Appalling."

"Odd kind of burglar. Looks like the only thing he pounced on were the books. Didn't seem to be interested in anything else."

"Have you been in the kitchen and bathroom?"

"Yes, I took pictures of everything. Seems tidy enough. But there weren't any books there."

"How did they get in? Are there any traces of the break-in?"

"None at all. They must be good at picking locks."

"Burglars usually are."

"What were they looking for in the books? Seems like they leafed through them before they were tossed."

He pointed at the tallest pile in the middle of the rug. Several of the volumes were lying open somewhere around the middle.

I shrugged. "What do burglars usually look for that can be put inside a book? Probably money."

"Who keeps money in books anymore?"

"Writers, for example. They think something is safest when they hide it in a book."

"Writers, sure. Your specialty. You were here last night, weren't you? What happened?"

"Nothing. Suspicions had been aroused that something was wrong with the woman who lives here. Apparently she was in the apartment, locked in from the inside, but was not answering the interphone or telephone. I didn't find anyone here."

"Had the door really been locked from the inside?"

"That's right."

"But how. . . .?"

I shrugged again.

"It looks like we won't know until we find the woman."

"How did you get in?"

"Inspector Vesić opened it for me."

"Of course. Nothing stands in his way." He hesitated a moment as though uncertain and then asked, "Are you sure you locked it on your way out?"

I nodded. "Quite certain. Inspector Vesić would have told me if I hadn't. He would not have allowed such an oversight."

"This doesn't seem to be an ordinary break-in. If the burglar really was looking for money, as you say, they were certainly counting on a tidy sum, what with all this effort. They would've had to have been here a long time to check each book. When did you leave here?"

"A little after eleven." I decided not to mention my second visit. Further explanation would be required and I didn't feel like going into the details right then.

"They probably had enough time the rest of the night. But there's another problem. Judging by the disorder," his free hand swept over the scattered books, "they didn't take much account of the noise they made. Like they didn't care if the neighbors heard. There's nothing quiet about throwing heavy books on the floor. But no one heard anything. Inspector Zarić went one floor down and checked it out."

"Maybe they're sound sleepers."

"No one sleeps that soundly. You'd have had to be deaf not to hear this."

I snapped my fingers when the word "deaf" reminded me of something.

"I know someone who would have heard even much softer sounds. He has a perfect sense of hearing."

Without any more ado, I turned around and left Miss Jakovljević's apartment. Inspector Zarić was now standing alone in front of it. He gave me a puzzled look as I silently took two steps to the other side of the corridor and raised my hand to the doorbell, thinking how much easier life was during daylight than at night.

Before my index finger reached the button, the door started to open. The person who appeared was not Mr. Teodosijević, however, but the one I least expected. Although, naturally, I should have.

$\curlyvee$ 15 $\curlyvee$

"GOOD MORNING, INSPECTOR LUKIĆ," said Commissioner Milenković. "You overslept."

He looked like he had not slept a wink. There were visible circles under his eyes and his tie was a little crooked. But he was freshly shaven.

"Good morning," I replied after a brief pause. "I didn't oversleep. My shift began at nine."

"If you stick to shifts you miss a lot in a policeman's line of work. And if you get a lot of sleep. While you were resting, things here were jumping."

He motioned his head toward Miss Jakovljević's apartment.

"It seems that even a service without shifts that never sleeps was unable to prevent the break-in."

"We don't cover break-ins."

"Not even when it's the apartment of someone you're interested in?"

The commissioner glanced over my shoulder at Inspector Zarić and, moving aside, opened the door fully.

"Come on in."

There was a young woman in the large room who could not have been more than twenty-six or -seven. If I had run into her in the street I would never have thought that she worked for the National Security Agency. Her dark hair was shaved above her ears and the rest of her head was covered with multicolored streaks. She had little rings in the middle of her lower lip and on the edge of her left nostril, and two more larger rings hung from her earlobes. She was wearing skin-tight jeans that were ripped in a few places, a colorful knit vest that barely reached her navel and a white wide-collared shirt with sleeves rolled up to just below the elbow.

Judging by this girl and the young man I had met the night before in the Communications Department, one would say that the Agency had brought in fresh blood and changed style. I did not recall anyone younger than forty among Commissioner Milenković's earlier associates, and you could more or less tell what they did for a living by their conduct and dress code. Compared to this new generation, the commissioner alone gave this impression now, although he was still quite inconspicuous as someone whose main concern was national security. Perhaps it was time he retired. Or perhaps he was one of those irreplaceable people who keep on working even after they retire.

The girl was taking photographs of the framed paintings that densely covered the walls. As I entered the room she turned, quickly raised her camera and took my picture.

"I didn't have time to smile," I said with a belated smile.

"I already have a picture of you smiling," she replied, also smiling, then went back to her work without offering any explanation.

Everything in the large room looked the same as it had the night before: the cot under the window, the brown armchair facing it, and the tall round stool next to the easel in the middle with a covered painting on it. The easel no longer stood out because the bright ceiling light was off. The apartment faced northwest so it did not get much morning light. I walked toward the large opening in the partition wall and looked into the small room.

"We're alone, Inspector Lukić," said Commissioner Milenković behind me.

"What about Mr. Teodosijević?" I asked, turning to face him.

"He's on a trip. Abroad."

I gazed at him, mystified. "He left this morning?"

"No. He's been gone for three weeks and will stay at least another three."

"How's that possible? I talked to him last night."

Commissioner Milenković took a large cellphone out of his inside jacket pocket, punched some buttons and then raised it toward me.

"Is this the person you talked to?"

I moved my head a little closer to get a better look at the photograph on the screen. The man bore no resemblance to the one I had seen the night before. His eyes were even more different than his facial features. They were muddy-brown and watery, the exact opposite of sparkling jade.

"Who is that?" I asked, although there was no need.

"Mr. Branislav Teodosijević. Artist. The owner of this atelier. They are three hours ahead of us where he is so we didn't wake him when we called this morning to ask permission to enter here."

"I don't understand," I said, shaking my head. "Then who was the man who introduced himself as Teodosijević?"

"I'd like to know that too. No one in our database matches his description."

I wrinkled my brow. "How do you know what he looks like?"

"That at least was not hard to find out. You weren't the only one here last night."

"Miss Aksentijević. . . ."

The corners of Commissioner Milenković's lips

turned up almost imperceptibly. "She was very willing to cooperate, even though we did wake her up."

"Why did you wake her up?"

"To check whether you might have neglected to tell us something about what happened here last night. For example, you made no mention of meeting the painter."

"I didn't consider it important. I didn't think it had any connection with the telephone that made our paths cross again."

Commissioner Milenković sighed. "In this work it's always wiser to assume there's some connection. In any case, Miss Aksentijević mentioned him right away and helped us determine what he looks like. It turns out she has an excellent eye for detail. Here, see for yourself."

His fingers danced over the buttons on the cellphone's little keypad once more, then he raised it toward me. If I didn't know it was a computer-generated composite portrait, I would have sworn I had a photograph of the alleged Mr. Teodosijević in front of me.

"Does it bear a resemblance?" said Commissioner Milenković, more as a statement than a question.

I nodded. "Very much."

"Miss Aksentijević said she immediately distrusted him. One might say she was more astute than an inspector."

"Is that so? What was it that raised her suspicions?"

"The fact that he was blind, of course. Or even that he was impersonating a blind man and introduced himself as a painter."

"If there have been deaf composers and illiterate writers, why not a blind painter?" I stopped for a moment and looked around the large room. The girl was still hard at work taking pictures, paying no attention to us. "If I had any doubts like Miss Aksentijević, they disappeared when I saw these paintings. This is exactly how I imagined a blind man would paint. . . ."

"That's not much of a compliment to the real Teodosijević. Well, let's not go into that right now. As you know, art is not my forte. I'm more interested in what else you can say about the man you met here last night. Miss Aksentijević saw him only briefly, and you met him one more time, right?"

We looked at each other in silence for a few moments.

"You are well informed, even without a cooperating eyewitness," I said.

"I have traces that, as a rule, are more reliable than eyewitnesses. Last night, just after you left the Communications Department, Mr. Teodosijević called you through your duty officer to tell you that someone was in Miss Jakovljević's apartment. You stayed in the building over half an hour. You didn't need that long to inspect the little neighboring apartment. It doesn't take much hard thinking to realize that you spent most of the time talking to the alleged blind painter. That must have been in here, right? Why would you stand in the corridor?"

"I see you know how long I was in the building."

"Of course I know. Did you expect me not to put an immediate tail on the man who had such a strange cellphone?"

"Even when he's a fellow inspector?"

"Especially when I've already had unforgettable experience with this same fellow inspector."

"Bearing that experience in mind, I'd say it would be useful for both of us if we cooperated. This time, however, not one-way. . . ."

We looked each other in the eye again briefly. Two clicks of the camera were all that disturbed the silence. Finally, Commissioner Milenković gestured toward the armchair.

"Take a seat," he said and then headed for the cot. He sat down next to the metal frame where Adam's owner had been the night before. He waited for me to get settled and then asked: "What would you like to know?"

"I assume you had the building under surveillance the whole night. What happened while I was peacefully asleep?"

"Nothing."

"What do you mean, nothing?"

"No one went in or out of the building after you left at 00:52 until this morning at 07:26 when the cleaning woman arrived."

"Is there any other way out except the main entrance?"

"There's one in the back." He pointed his thumb over his shoulder at the window behind his back. "There's a little park. No one was there either."

"So where could the false Teodosijević be?"

"Not only him but his dog too. The simplest answer is that if they didn't leave the building then they must still be in it. But that doesn't seem very probable."

"Why not?"

The shadow of a smile crossed Commissioner Milenković's face again. "How about if I do the asking for a bit? We've done away with the one-way cooperation if I'm not mistaken."

"Go ahead," I replied contritely.

"What did you find when you visited Miss Jakovljević's apartment the second time?"

"The same as the first. No one was there."

"What did the allegedly blind painter say about that?"

"He said I was too late. The visitor had purportedly left before I got there."

"Was there any trace of them?"

"Not that I noticed."

"Did you take something with you again, by any chance?"

I shook my head and replied with a question: "What would I take?"

Before I finished my sentence I felt a vibration in my pants pocket announcing that I had received a message. I knew it could not be seen and would stop very quickly, but even so I interlaced my fingers more hastily than I intended and put both hands over my pant leg. As though things were not tense enough already, the girl turned toward me suddenly and took another picture. Once again her only explanation was a smile.

"I don't know," said Commissioner Milenković, shrugging his shoulders. "I thought there might be other unusual devices such as a cellphone without a SIM card and battery."

"I didn't see anything unusual. Everything looked the same as the first time."

"Then the mysterious visitor was incomparably more discreet than the one that came afterward and made that mess with the books. If, of course, there was any visitor."

"What do you mean?"

"Perhaps the impostor in Teodosijević the painter's apartment used the excuse of a nonexistent visitor to lure you back here again."

"Since he was an impostor, wouldn't he rather see the back of a police inspector instead of luring him here again?"

"That would be more natural, I agree. Unless he had some special reason to see this very same police inspector in private."

"What might that reason be?" I asked after a brief hesitation.

"I can't imagine. Something, however, certainly kept you talking for almost half an hour. What did you talk about?"

I gazed at him again without speaking.

"I think my turn has come to ask questions," I replied at last.

Commissioner Milenković seemed about to protest, but then he just nodded.

"Go ahead."

"What are you doing here in Mr. Teodosijević's apartment?"

"Is it hard to guess? There's no better stakeout for Miss Jakovljević's apartment. It's a shame we didn't come last night, things would probably be much clearer now. We entered as soon as the cleaning lady reported the break-in. If we'd found someone in the apartment, we would have talked them into cooperating. It turned out simpler this way, even though a new mystery cropped up. But at least we established that the Teodosijević here was a fake. And the real one's mind is now at rest. He would have a hard time finding a better guard for his apartment than the National Security Agency."

"Have you been to Miss Jakovljević's?"

"Just briefly." He nodded toward the girl. "There was only enough time to take a few pictures. Your colleagues got here quickly."

"The cleaning lady must have seen you."

"Yes, but we had no trouble convincing her that she hadn't."

I smiled. "She's quite credible when she says she didn't see anyone."

"All right," said Commissioner Milenković, keeping a straight face. "Let's get back to my question. What did you talk about?"

I pressed my interlaced fingers more firmly over my pants pocket.

"The Grand Manuscript," I said in a low voice.

He grabbed the root of his nose between his thumb and index finger, closed his eyes and bowed his head a little. As I looked at him in that position, he seemed like an old man for the first time. An old man surrounded by adversity. He sighed noisily through his nose, then spoke softly as well, without raising his head.

"I'm listening."

"It's a twisted story. Everything revolves around Miss Jakovljević's new novel. She writes detective stories. It seems that some people believe it is a . . . special . . . book. Apparently, the first one to read it will become—immortal."

Commissioner Milenković let go of his nasal root and raised his head.

"Immortal?" he repeated without any special emphasis.

"I told you it was twisted. Literature sometimes has peculiar side effects. . . ."

"You're telling me. . . ." he mumbled with another sigh.

"I don't think anything . . . out of the ordinary . . . is about to happen. Last night you mentioned Occam's razor. The simplest explanation is that Miss Jakovljević has gone somewhere to finish her new book in peace so the weirdos don't bother her. She didn't even ask us for protection. If someone hadn't been searching her apartment last night, the police would have had no reason to get involved."

"If only Occam's razor could always be applied. How, for example, did Miss Jakovljević leave an apartment that was locked from the inside? By the way, what did Inspector Vesić have to say about that?"

"He was impressed."

Commissioner Milenković nodded.

"There, you see. But a cellphone that works without a SIM card and battery is an even greater mystery."

"Didn't you say that communications technology is coming up with new things all the time?"

"I did. This, however, would be a real communications revolution, and I doubt that the first we heard of it would come from a woman who writes detective books and is being hounded by weirdos. But there's a third mystery that's giving me the biggest headache."

"Third mystery?"

Frowning, Commissioner Milenković rubbed his temples with the tips of his fingers and turned his head toward the girl.

"Officer, if you please. . . ."

The photographer lowered her camera, went up to the easel and with a sharp jerk removed the cloth covering the painting.

∽ 16 ∾

IF IT HAD BEEN anyone else, I would have recognized him at once. Provided, of course, that I knew him. As it was, it took at least two seconds for me to realize that I was looking at my own smiling face. The photographer must have had this in mind when she'd said she already had a picture of me smiling.

Incredulous, I got up from the squeaky armchair and went to the easel in the middle of the room. It was a sketch on a large square piece of paper pinned to the frame. Drawn in short strokes with charcoal, I would say it had been done in a hurry, but that was only a guess. In any case, it had been made by someone very skilled at drawing. Although just an outline, it was a perfect likeness. I didn't have a single painting or drawing of myself, so I would have loved to frame this one and put it in my study, but it would do no good to ask Commissioner Milenković. Even if the case were quickly closed, the National Security Agency would never part with evidence.

Instead of going back to work, the girl remained next to the easel and took pictures of me staring at myself. I turned toward her; I could tell by the upturned corners of her mouth that she was amused by my confusion.

I looked at Commissioner Milenković. "Who drew this?"

"Not Mr. Teodosijević."

"Did you ask him?"

"Yes. He was almost insulted."

"Why?"

"First of all, he's never seen you. At least that's what he claims. And then, it seems he's not a fan of figurative painting. To put it mildly."

"Is that so?"

"Why does that surprise you?" His hand gestured toward the walls covered with black and red arabesques. "It was to be expected."

"So who drew it if he didn't?"

"The choice is not very wide, at least as far as we know."

"The false Mr. Teodosijević? Even if he had a talent for drawing, he couldn't have made my portrait because he couldn't see me."

"Are you certain?"

"What? He was blind so he couldn't have made my portrait or he was blind so he couldn't see me?"

"The latter. The former would not surprise me. There is little that can still surprise me so far as artists are concerned. Who knows, maybe a blind painter would be able to draw you based on your voice."

"You overestimate artists. If he relied solely on my voice, the result would be something like the paintings on the walls. If, however, he was only pretending to be blind, then he was very convincing."

Commissioner Milenković nodded his head. "He is without doubt a master of deception."

"Judging by that, it seems that not even you know what happened to him after we said goodbye last night. Where are he and the dog if your people didn't see them leave the building? Does it have anything to do with the break-in at Miss Jakovljević's apartment?"

"Those are all very interesting questions, Inspector Lukić. One of them, however, intrigues me more than the others. And worries me too."

He got up, went to the easel and gazed at the drawing. In the meantime, the girl had gone into the small room where clicking could be heard from time to time.

"Which one?" I asked to snap him out of his musing.

The commissioner knocked with his index finger on the edge of the drawing paper.

"Why is it a portrait of you?"

I shrugged. "I have no idea."

Just as I said this, the cell in my pants pocket started vibrating again. I barely stopped myself from reflexively covering the pocket with my hand. But it was even harder to bear up under the commissioner's inquisitive look.

"Absolutely nothing comes to mind?"

We were standing less than a meter apart, looking each other straight in the eye. The clicking stopped in the small room.

I shook my head. "Nothing."

The commissioner examined me again briefly, then sighed audibly through his nose. He took the cloth from the easel trestle and covered the drawing.

"I expect you to call me if you think of anything. Now we're cooperating fully, aren't we?"

"To be sure. I hope that you will contact me in the same spirit if something comes up. For example, if you get onto the alleged Mr. Teodosijević's trail."

"To be sure, to be sure," replied Commissioner Milenković with a tinge of impatience. "Cooperation above all."

I motioned my head toward the front door. "I don't suppose you have anything against us sealing Miss Jakovljević's apartment. Those are regulations, as you know, although the measure is not necessary, of course. The writer, along with the painter, currently has the safest apartment in town."

"Goodbye, Inspector Lukić."

Inspectors Kostić and Zarić were waiting for me in

the corridor with questioning looks, but they didn't ask anything. I went to the door of the neighboring apartment, took out the key and locked it twice. The key moved smoothly in the lock.

"Seal this, please," I said to Inspector Kostić.

He turned briefly toward the door to the painter's apartment, as though in a quandary, then nodded. He opened his equipment bag, having already placed his camera inside, squatted by the door to Miss Jakovljević's apartment and got to work. It took him less than three minutes to finish.

"There's not enough room for all three of us," I said when we were in front of the door to the little elevator. "I'll take the stairs."

Kostić and Zarić exchanged quick looks and then headed after me. I had hoped they would take the elevator. This was a new chance to count the steps at my leisure, in daylight. But it didn't work. I doubted they would keep quiet until the ground floor.

Inspector Zarić was the first to speak, softly, when we reached the fourth floor.

"This must be something big if Commissioner Milenković is here in person."

"Must be," I replied in a low voice.

"He kept you a long time," said Inspector Kostić, half as a query.

"He wanted to know what happened here last night."

"Who would think," said Zarić, "that the Agency would be interested in . . . an authoress. . . ."

I would not have responded if the last two words had not been spoken derisively.

"That's because they've brought in new blood. The old guys aren't readers, while these younger ones are well-read. They won't hire them otherwise. Rumor has it that being well-read will soon be a requirement for us too. Haven't you heard? How's your reading coming along, you two?"

The inspectors exchanged glances again.

"So-so. . . ." replied Kostić.

"My advice is that you get cracking right away. It doesn't have to be serious reading matter. Take detective novels, for example. That's something you know. You could even start with Miss Jakovljević. If the Agency finds her interesting, I'm sure you will too."

"What would you recommend?" asked Zarić.

Serves me right, I thought. The predicament I'd gotten myself into only worsened when the cellphone started trembling in my pocket again. This was getting stressful. As I pretended to mull it over, we reached the ground floor. Officer Vranešević rushed out of the foyer and held the door open for us.

"Whichever of Miss Jakovljević's eight books you choose, you won't be wrong," I said in front of the building. "They are all excellent."

They nodded and then climbed into the back seat of the patrol car. Vranešević got behind the wheel and had already started the car when I remembered something and knocked on the window. Kostić opened it.

"Send those pictures you took upstairs to my computer right away, please."

"All right."

I took a look around after the patrol car left. Even though it was almost ten o'clock, the short street was empty. Heading for my car, I closely examined Miss Jakovljević's apartment along the way. Not only her windows, but all those on this side of the building were full of brightly reflected sunlight. Just as I inserted the key in the car door, barking disrupted the calm Saturday morning. I raised my head in the direction from which it had come and caught sight of a large dog at the far corner of the street. It looked at me and continued to bark, as though wanting to draw my attention. As soon as it was certain I had seen it, the dog turned and disappeared down a side street.

I quickly took out the key and started running. This certainly must have confused Commissioner Milenković's invisible people, assigned to monitor my every move, but that was not important just then. I had to double check. All German shepherds look more or less the same to me, particularly when seen briefly and from a distance. It was probably just a stray dog, but it might have been Adam.

I reached the corner in a jiffy and looked down the street, which was longer than Oak Street. Out of five pedestrians, the two closest to me turned around, attracted by the sound of my running, and looked in bewilderment as I stood there turning my head left and right, clearly searching for someone. I was bewildered too. There was no dog anywhere in sight.

I waited for the curious pedestrians to continue on their way and then carried on down the street at a normal pace, looking all around. The dog had to be nearby, out of sight somewhere. This would have been easier, of course, had the dog been smaller. There were not many places where a big dog could fit. And why would it first lure me this way and then hide, as though we were playing hide-and-seek?

I didn't feel like playing, so I stopped after five or six steps, determined to go back. That's when I caught sight of the wrought iron fence several buildings away. The dog might be there. Three tall steps led down to the teashop's below-level entrance—quite enough space for even a person to take cover if they crouched low.

Approaching it cautiously, I looked down through the railings. There was no one in front of the entrance. I shrugged my shoulders and turned to go back, then thought, why not stop by, since I was already there. The shot putter had invited me to come back when I was not with Miss Aksentijević. Here was that chance. I was not in a hurry to go anywhere.

~ 17 ~

As I descended the steps, it crossed my mind that the teashop might not be open this early on a Saturday. There was no sign on the door with its opening hours. I pulled down on the massive iron handle and at first thought it was locked, but then the door started to move and, as on the day before, herbal fragrances greeted me from the semi-darkness. Even on a bright day not much sunlight penetrated; the lower halves of the two windows were always in shadow.

I remained in the entrance for several moments, waiting for my eyes to adjust to the subdued light. Even then all I could really see was the illuminated wall opposite me with the bar. Next to it stood a middle-aged man with luxuriant curly hair in a white shirt and brown vest, busy with the cups and saucers. The muted music was drowned out by the sound of water running in the sink. He raised his head toward me and nodded with a smile.

"Good morning," he said in a soft voice, turning off the water.

"Good morning," I replied. "I hope I'm not too early."

"Certainly not. We open at nine. Every day. Please take a seat, sir."

As I looked around the teashop, I realized it was not empty as I had first thought. On the left, approximately in the middle of the wall, someone was sitting on the dark-brown leather banquette, but I could not tell whether it was a man or a woman. The contours of a cup were on the table.

I headed for the little round table where I had sat the night before with Miss Aksentijević. The waiter wiped his hands and then approached me, smiling all the while. He minced his steps as though wearing high heels, even though his shoes were flat. There was a brass pin in the shape of a teapot on the lapel of his vest.

"Tea against illusions is to your liking, sir, if I'm not mistaken?"

I looked at him warily. "Does it show?"

"No, it does not show, but we know. We keep track of our customers. That's the tea you had last night. I hope that it helped you."

I shook my head. "I'm afraid not. I'm still plagued by illusions. I just had one a few minutes ago."

"Then we'll have to add something to your tea." His smile broadened. "Sometimes we don't get the remedy right the first time."

He hastened back to the bar, swinging his hips.

Watching as he prepared the tea with theatrical movements, I wondered what the Agency people tailing me thought about everything that had happened in the past ten minutes. First I had run after a dog, then the dog had disappeared without a trace and I'd ended up in the teashop where they had no surveillance. More customers could be expected at any moment. What tea would suit them? What would be their complaints?

A thought suddenly struck me and I looked over my left shoulder at the middle of the wall that was now behind my back. My vision had improved somewhat, but I still could not make out the person sitting there. I was certainly more visible to them because I was close to the window. I faced forward again so my staring would not be conspicuous.

Nevertheless, no, I concluded. Even though Commissioner Milenković was certainly not to be underestimated, that would be going too far. They had no reason to keep someone in the teashop. Nothing had indicated that I would stop by. I had not even known it myself. If I let paranoia get the upper hand, I would end up seeing Agency people everywhere. Even the waiter who was just bringing me my tea.

He placed the cup in front of me.

"This should get rid of your illusions."

"The woman who served me yesterday must have given you a good description if you recognized me so easily."

"There was no need to describe you. I had a good look at you last night. I was really curious to see what the customer looked like who asked for tea against illusions. It's not ordered very often." He swept a curl off his forehead. "And one does not forget such a nice manly face. . . ."

"You see quite well in this dim light. I can barely make things out. And Madam was truly admirable in that regard."

"Miss, actually. My sister."

I looked at him closely.

"I might be wrong, but I wouldn't say you resemble each other very much."

"We don't resemble each other at all. As you know, she is quite. . . .butch."

"I thought she did athletics. Some throwing event. . . ."

"She's done different jobs. Mostly men's. Now she's settled down here. Teas are her strong suit. It's a family trait."

"Last night we started an interesting conversation, but didn't have a chance to finish it. When will she be in the teashop again?"

"From five in the afternoon to one in the morning. We will be pleased to see you again. Me in particular . . . And we have to check whether the illusions are gone. Enjoy your tea, sir."

The tea now seemed a deeper red. That might have been owing to the new ingredients or the influence of spare daylight. I brought the white bell-shaped steaming cup to my lips and sipped the hot liquid carefully. A sweetish taste now joined the bitter and sour that I remembered from the night before. As I lowered my cup, vibrations filled my pocket once again.

I hastened to take out the black cellphone. Finally I had a chance to read the messages. This was the fourth. Coming to the teashop had turned out to be rather a good idea. Reading the messages in the car, office or any other public place would not have been wise; that would not have escaped the attention of those who were tailing me. Then I would have had a hard time explaining to Commissioner Milenković which cell I had used when there was no trace of my service or private phone. I turned briefly once again to the invisible person behind my back. I should be safe here.

I pressed a button on the keypad and the last message appeared on the screen.

"If this were a detective novel, Inspector Lukić, it would be high time you checked the messages you receive on this special telephone. There is no compelling narrative coherence that could explain your ignoring them."

I wanted to reply at once, but opened the three previous messages first.

"What should we do now?"

That was the first one. I had received it after Commissioner Milenković asked whether I might have taken something else from Miss Jakovljević's apartment.

"You really have no idea? Pretty poor intuition for a police inspector. . . ."

The second message had come after I replied to the Commissioner's question as to why my portrait had been drawn that I had no idea.

"It's certainly no compliment when someone recommends a writer without reading a single one of their books. . . ."

The third message had come after Inspector Zarić's awkward question regarding which of Miss Jakovljević's books I would recommend.

I thought things over for a few moments and then opened the last message again, chose Reply and started to write.

"If this were a detective novel, the writer would not complicate the inspector's life by sending unimportant messages at the most inconvenient times. There is certainly even less compelling narrative coherence for her playing tricks."

A new message arrived just a moment after I had sent mine.

"If you had read any of the writer's books you would know that playing tricks is her distinctive trait. And it has excellent narrative coherence."

"Coherent or not, it's an obstruction. I'm tempted to turn off this cell."

"It isn't easy to turn off a cell without a battery. . . ."

"Maybe so, but I could stop taking it with me."

"Under no circumstances would I advise that you stay out of contact with the writer. Her help might come in very handy."

"Is it commonplace in your novels for the writer to help the inspector?"

"No, it only happens when the inspector can't find his bearings. Like you, for instance."

"I can't find my bearings?"

"That's what it looks like. You're trying to find the writer's trail, aren't you?"

"Yes."

"And you don't even know what she looks like. Isn't that indispensable? You might run into her without realizing who she is. . . ."

As I feverishly considered what to reply, the service phone in my jacket started ringing. Rattled, for a few moments I did not know what to do with the phone in my hand. I finally put it back in my pants pocket and reached into my left inside jacket pocket.

"Hello!" I said, almost shouting.

"Is everything all right?" asked Inspector Prokopović, mystified.

"Yes, yes," I hastened to assure him. "Just a little . . . hitch. . . ."

"Do you plan on coming over here soon?"

"Yes, I was just getting ready to go. Why?"

"You have a visitor."

"Who is it?"

"A lawyer from Search Publishers."

"Since when do lawyers work on Saturday?"

"I don't know, but if I were you, I wouldn't waste a moment."

"It's that urgent?"

"No, that's how good she looks. It's almost a sin to make such a pretty woman wait. . . ."

Just like the night before when the alleged painter Teodosijević had called about the break-in at Miss Jakovljević's apartment, I wanted to ask at least three questions at once, but instead I just replied: "I'm on my way."

I put my service phone back in my jacket pocket and finished my tea as I got up. It had cooled while I was exchanging messages. The ones I received had come in a split second, unlike the ones I composed that were so frustratingly slow, even though I wrote quickly. I headed for the bar with long strides, taking change out of my pocket along the way.

"It's not a good idea to let tea go cold and then drink it all at once," said the tea maker reprovingly. "It has the best medicinal effect while it's hot. Besides, tea should be a pleasure." He stopped briefly and his seemingly stern expression turned into an impish smile. "As should life. . . ."

I sighed. "Obligations spoil pleasure. With tea and with life. . . ."

"You must be swamped with obligations. Being an inspector isn't easy, I imagine."

I looked at him askance. "Is this another family trait—guessing your customers' profession—or is it just your sister who is endowed and you found out from her?"

"I found out from my sister, although I could have

guessed by myself. We both have that skill. And I'm sure you have it too. How could a police inspector not be well-endowed. . . .?"

We looked at each other for a moment in silence. A curl had fallen on his forehead again and he twisted it around his index finger.

"You overrate police inspectors," I said. "You and your sister, for example, might have an easy time guessing the profession of your other customer, but I couldn't do it at all."

"What other customer?"

I motioned with my head to the left. "That one."

The tea maker looked in that direction and then questioningly at me. I turned around quickly and stared at the place where I had seen someone sitting. The light was still dim over there, but the banquette along the wall and the chairs next to the little round table were definitely empty. I looked around the teashop in bewilderment.

"It seems we'll have to add something more to your tea against illusions, Inspector," said the tea maker with another grin. "I look forward to seeing you again tonight."

⌒ 18 ⌒

It was not customary for an unannounced visitor to wait in an inspector's office. There was a common waiting room on the ground floor, but the duty officer at the entrance probably thought it was not elegant enough for such a lady. Her looks even made me ashamed of my office, which had never happened before. Perhaps not even the chief inspector's office would have suited her.

She was sitting in the armchair facing my desk with her long legs crossed. Everything about her was stylish: black pants and a blazer with discreet pinstripes, a dark-red wide collar blouse, open to the fourth button, shoes of the same color with a medium heel and a row of decorative little straps. The handkerchief sprouting like a bouquet from the left breast pocket of her blazer matched her blouse.

High cheekbones made her large blue eyes look a little slanted. She did not require a toothy smile to appear cheerful. Her coal-black hair was luxuriant, straight, parted in the middle, reaching just below her ears. She was barely over thirty so there was almost no need for makeup.

"Sorry to keep you waiting," I said, pausing before her. No apology was called for, but that's how it sounded.

"It's no problem. You didn't know I was coming."

She held out her hand. Her handshake was firm despite her seemingly delicate hands. Then she reached into the inside pocket of her blazer and handed me a business card.

"Jovana Timotijević, attorney at law."

"Inspector Dejan Lukić," I replied, putting the card on my desk. "What business brings you to the police station on a Saturday morning, Mrs. Timotijević?"

"Miss. . . ." she said, correcting me.

"Excuse me . . . Miss. . . ."

"Urgent business, Inspector. I hope that you can spare me a little of your time."

"With pleasure."

She gave me a smile but did not continue, and looked at me as though expecting something. I returned the look, perplexed.

"There's no need for you to stand while we talk," she said at last. "It won't be quite that quick."

"Of course," I said with a nod, feeling foolish.

As I hastened around the desk to take my seat, Miss Timotijević opened the large black briefcase she had placed on the floor next to the armchair. She took out a piece of paper and handed it to me.

"My power of attorney."

"Thank you." I skimmed over the short text and gave it back to her.

"I have been informed that you are in charge of Miss Jakovljević's missing person case."

I shook my head. "You have been incorrectly informed. I am in charge of no such case."

Now she looked at me in bewilderment.

"You're not?"

"The police are not investigating Miss Jakovljlević's disappearance."

"Didn't you . . . break into . . . her apartment last night?"

"Your source is unreliable. There was no break-in."

"What would you call it, then, when the police enter a private apartment without authorization?"

"No authorization was required. Your source was the one who reported that Miss Jakovljević was locked inside her apartment and something might be wrong with her. As someone well-acquainted with the law, you undoubtedly know that in such cases the police have the right to enter an apartment without a court order. Even by force. Luckily, that was not necessary last night."

"Be that as it may, you didn't find Miss Jakovljević in the apartment?"

"No, I didn't."

"And the door was locked from the inside?"

"That's right."

"Isn't that sufficient grounds for the police to investigate her disappearance?"

"No, it isn't. The police are not interested in whether apartment owners lock their doors from the outside or inside when they leave, or where they go afterward."

I could tell by the movement of her blue eyes that she was thinking quickly.

"So does that mean that as far as the police are concerned, there is no Miss Jakovljević case?"

"There is, but only as of this morning."

"This morning?"

"Last night, actually. During the night someone really did break into her apartment and ransacked it. We found out this morning."

Her eyes were now calm as she surveyed me in silence.

"Did they steal . . . anything?"

"I don't know. Only Miss Jakovljević would be able to say."

She lowered her eyes so I could not see them during the brief silence that followed.

"What about you?" she said, suddenly raising her head. "Did you find . . . anything . . . when you entered the apartment last night?"

"Such as what?" I retorted.

"Anything at all."

"I didn't find anything."

"Did you turn on her computer?"

"I had no reason to. Miss Jakovljević could not have been hiding inside it."

She seemed tempted to say something about my sense of humor, but held back.

"Did you go into the apartment after the break-in?"

"Yes."

"Was the computer still there?"

I thought for a moment and then nodded my head. "Yes."

"Was it turned on or off?"

"Off." I stopped for a moment. "You certainly are interested in Miss Jakovljević's computer. . . ."

She did not reply at once. Her deep-blue eyes scrutinized me. Then she reached into her briefcase again. This time she took out a sheaf of papers stapled together.

"It's not the computer that interests me but what's inside it. The file with Miss Jakovljević's new novel. It is the property of my client."

She folded back the first sheet and handed me the document. It was some kind of contract. Parts of the text were redacted.

"Article Four," said Miss Timotijević. "The manuscript is the sole property of Search Publishers."

I quickly read the three paragraphs of Article Four.

"Does this cover just the finished manuscript?" I asked.

"It covers any form of the manuscript, particularly when it's finished. Please understand the circumstances. My client paid Miss Jakovljević a very large advance. . . ."

"That's what's been blacked out, right?" I said, interrupting her, and handed her back the document.

"Yes. It's confidential information that concerns the contracting parties alone and is not for other eyes. But believe me, it's truly enormous."

"I never imagined that truly enormous sums were part of the local publishing industry."

"Miss Jakovljević is a very popular writer. In any case, the publisher is extremely interested in protecting his highly paid property. He definitely does not want anyone else to get their hands on the manuscript. Even briefly. It would cause inestimable damage."

"What kind of damage?"

She looked at me as though I'd asked a stupid question.

"It's not hard to divine. It's a detective novel. If someone malicious read the dénouement, they might leak how the book ends. On the internet, for example. Then no one would want to buy it. That would be a real catastrophe for the publisher."

"Couldn't they do same thing after the book comes out?"

"Yes, but then it would be too late. The major part of the print run is sold soon after the book hits the stores."

"Everything would be simpler if Miss Jakovljević didn't write detective novels."

"What do you mean, simpler?"

"Readers have yet to change their minds about buying serious literature because they know how the book ends."

"Perhaps. The publisher, however, makes his living selling detective novels, not serious literature. That's the only place where big money is at stake. And a possible big loss that we would consider the fault of those who should have prevented it, and didn't. The police, for example."

"The police cannot be expected to protect something if no one knows where it is."

"No one knows where it is? It has to be in the writer's computer. Where else would it be?"

"I have no idea, but it doesn't necessarily have to be in her computer. The mess in Miss Jakovljević's apartment confirms that."

"How?"

I returned her look of a moment ago.

"It's not hard to divine. If, as you think, last night's burglar really was someone malicious who did this just to damage your client, where is the first place they would look for the manuscript?"

"In her computer," she replied somewhat hesitantly, sensing trouble.

"That's right. But if they found it, they'd have no reason to ransack the apartment."

Her blue eyes started dancing again.

"Maybe they wanted to throw you off the scent. . . ."

"There was no need for that. If they'd got hold of the file, the smartest thing would be to leave as soon as possible and not draw attention with the noise that necessarily accompanies a ransacking. No, the file was not where you assumed it would be, and I'd say it wasn't anywhere else in Miss Jakovljević's apartment either. Judging by how the burglar left the apartment, they went away empty-handed."

"Maybe the file is somewhere in the apartment, but they didn't find it. . . ."

"Then you have no reason to worry. But the whole idea seems rather shaky—an ill-intentioned person pulling a risky break-in just to harm a publishing house. It's hard to imagine such a fanatic. This was much more likely an ordinary break-in. Writers who receive enormous fees have more chances of being robbed than mere mortals."

"It wasn't some fanatic or ordinary thief. Don't be naive. The burglar was hired to do it."

"Who hired them?"

"It's not hard to divine. Do you really know so little about how things work in the publishing world? Lots of publishers would loosen their purse strings to hurt the competition."

"I know so little because the publishers of the books I read have no need to resort to mafia tactics. . . ."

By the look on her face, she was hesitating whether to continue this battle of wits with me over highbrow and lowbrow literature. Finally, the attorney's expediency prevailed over her bruised ego.

"Shouldn't you be looking for Miss Jakovljević to tell her about the break-in at her apartment?"

"We have no idea where she might be and there are no grounds to issue an APB. She has committed no crime. All we can do is wait for her to turn up. That's how most such disappearances end anyway."

"If she turns up, please let me know immediately." She motioned her head toward the business card on the desk. "My client is very anxious to get hold of his property before other interested parties. Furthermore, please bear in mind how important it is that no one look at the manuscript." She paused briefly, then added with a hint of reluctance: "Not even you."

I smiled. "Don't worry, I certainly won't. I'm not a fan of novels that lose all value once you find out who did it."

Miss Timotijević took hold of her briefcase and stood up. I rose too. She was almost my height. The pants emphasized her long legs. She stretched out her hand across the desk. This time her firm handshake lasted a while.

"It was nice to meet you, Inspector Lukić." Her full lips turned up into a smile. "I'll find a way to personally repay you if you help me discover the file with Miss Jakovljević's new novel. As soon as possible."

Without waiting for me to reply, she finally let go of my hand, turned around gracefully and headed for the office door.

⌒ 19 ⌒

Before Miss Timotijević got to the elevator, the cellphone in my pocket started to vibrate again. I reached to take it out, but stopped at the last moment. Standing at the desk with my hand in my pocket, I looked around the office. There was no reason for those who had me under surveillance to be suspicious about my hand in my pocket. But this looking around would draw their attention. They might wonder what had led me to look for their surveillance camera at that particular moment. Good, let them rack their brains over it a bit.

They knew, of course, that I was on to them. Just as I knew that there was no sense in finding and disabling the hidden camera, because they would quickly install a new one in the same or another place, and my action would only increase their suspicions unnecessarily. Our cards were on the table. I knew they were watching me, they knew that I knew, and both sides knew that we would not stop trying to outwit each other in spite of our newly established two-way cooperation.

As I left my office, the elevator door was just closing after my visitor. I headed down the other side of the corridor. It was probably covered by cameras too, but not the place where I was going. Not even the National Security Agency would have the audacity to invade the privacy of the police men's room.

Everything in the stall was dark-green: the door, partition walls, tiles, toilet bowl. Even the lowered lid I was sitting on was a matching color. Before I took out the phone, I looked up briefly at the ceiling. It was predictably green too. No, even had they wanted, there was no way to hide a camera here. And they would need one for each of the six stalls. . . .

"So?" was the message.

"So?" I repeated.

"Stop pretending. How did the lady strike you?"

"She's pretty."

"That's all, pretty?"

"What else do you expect?"

"She usually leaves men breathless."

"This man held onto his breath. She's not my type."

"What is your type?"

"My current location is not exactly the right place to discuss that."

"You didn't have to go there. We could have freely exchanged messages even if you had stayed in your office."

"No we couldn't. There are too many curious eyes even when I'm alone. . . ."

"Let me worry about that. . . ."

"Oh, yes, I almost forgot. The almighty writer manipulates the world of the detective novel as she sees fit. But doesn't such meddling disrupt the narrative coherence behind the work?"

"It is less disruptive than an inspector going to the men's room all the time. Not to mention that the very next time might arouse the suspicions of curious eyes."

"Then the best thing is to spare the inspector from having to go to the men's room all the time. Everything would be fine without your messages."

"Am I forcing you to read them? Who's to blame for your own curiosity?"

"I could stop."

"That is what would endanger the narrative coherence. The inspector is given an exceptional telephone and then for no reason disregards the messages he receives on it."

"I don't have to take narrative coherence into account. I'm not a writer."

"But you are a smart inspector. Would you refuse the only trail that might lead to solving the case just out of a capricious desire to show that you can curb your curiosity?"

I stared at the message on the screen until it started to fade.

"I've already been here too long. The curious eyes will become suspicious."

"Just one more thing. If it had been Miss Jakovljević who just visited you, she would not have impressed you, then. . . ."

"It was Miss Timotijević, not Jakovljević."

"Are you sure? Any woman at all could show up with a false business card, power of attorney and contract. Should a police inspector be so credulous?"

I sighed before starting to write again.

"Now is the time to establish what the mysterious Miss Jakovljević looks like."

"Best of luck. . . ."

I put the phone back in my pants pocket and was just about to leave the stall when something occurred to me. There might not be hidden cameras in the men's room but why not a microphone? It would not be an invasion of privacy, and conversations sometimes took place there that might be of interest to the National Security Agency. I raised the lid and flushed the toilet. This should be sufficiently audible confirmation that I had come here for the usual reasons. I waited about half a minute, emerged and stopped briefly at the sink, washing my hands.

I sat down at my office desk and turned on the computer. The first thing it did was tell me that Inspector Kostić's photographs had arrived. They could wait. I opened my browser and wrote "Jelena Jakovljević" in Google. There were more than 150,000 hits. All of them certainly did not refer to the Jelena Jakovljević who interested me. It was not exactly an uncommon name. But a quick inspection revealed that the great majority were nonetheless about her. She seemed truly popular.

The writer's official website was at the top of the long list. I clicked on the link and entered the site. The first thing I expected to see was her picture, but it was missing. I went to the bottom of the page. Nothing there either. I went back to the beginning and after establishing that there was no picture anywhere, started to read the introduction. The very first sentence explained the absence of a photograph, but this only increased the mystery.

"Jelena Jakovljević" was a pseudonym. Since the real identity was not divulged, the lack of a picture was not surprising. The real author of eight detective novels had to hide their appearance so no one would recognize them. I stared pensively at the screen where shades of brown prevailed. Then I put the cursor back in the Google field in the upper right-hand corner of the screen and added "pseudonym" after "Jelena Jakovljević".

The number of hits this time was much smaller, but still rather large. Readers were clearly intrigued as to who was hiding behind the pseudonym. I visited several of numerous forums that discussed this topic. Excluding the frivolity characteristic of anonymous collocutors exchanging ideas on the internet, the prevailing belief was that the pseudonym belonged to a reputable author of highbrow literature who was embarrassed by their forays into detective fiction.

It was interesting to see that by far the majority of candidates proposed were male. The assumption of such literary cross-dressing made me smile, particularly when I saw the names most mentioned. But whoever had resorted to the pseudonym was not a man. Miss Aksentijević spoke of the author she represented as a woman, and there would be no sense in doing so if the person was of the opposite sex. Why would she needlessly confuse the inspector she expected to find her client?

It was not clear, however, why she had called her by her pseudonym. Did she count on the police doing their job without learning the real identity of the missing writer? The fact that they would see her did not have to mean that they recognized her. She might not be a public figure at all. The other possibility would be that Miss Aksentijević did not even know who was hiding behind "Jelena Jakovljević". Yes, but then there were the contracts. Her real name probably had to be written there. Or did it? It was a shame I hadn't looked in more detail at the document Miss Timotijević had briefly shown me. Unless, of course, the name had been also censored as confidential information.

In either case, Miss Aksentijević might not know who Jelena Jakovljević was, but she certainly knew what she looked like. And she had proved talented at describing someone she had seen briefly only once. Commissioner Milenković might have asked her to describe the writer, but I doubted it. He had no grounds. Nothing had led him—or me, for that matter—to suspect that her identity was shrouded in mystery.

I searched through my pockets until I found the business card that Miss
Aksentijević had given me the night before and then took out my service cellphone. As I pressed the buttons, I had a notion that this was not going to be an easy conversation, bearing in mind her mood when

we had parted. But I had no choice. Who else could describe the person who presented themselves as Jelena Jakovljević the writer? The fake painter Teodosijević claimed that he had talked to her, but it was hard to believe him in any regard, and he had disappeared so masterfully that not even the Agency could find any trace of him.

The telephone started to ring. If it turned out that Miss Aksentijević was still peeved with me, all I had left was Miss Timotijević, although she did not raise my hopes very much. Judging by what I had learned in the teashop the night before, the writer's agent was the primary contact with the publisher. If Miss Aksentijević was authorized to sign contracts or if she took them to her client to be signed, it was possible that Miss Timotijević had never seen the person who had made a name for themselves as Jelena Jakovljević.

Just when I thought she wouldn't answer, after the seventh ring I finally heard her groggy voice.

"Hello."

"Hello. Inspector Dejan Lukić speaking."

Silence reigned for several long moments.

"Good morning," she said like it was the last thing she meant.

"Did I wake you?"

"This is the second time the police have wakened me on a Saturday morning. The secret police did it at the crack of dawn. It wasn't even eight. I barely got back to sleep after they left and now you've done your best to ruin that. I'll be good for nothing all day, drowsy like this."

"Should I not have called with news for you?"

"If your news is as bad as this morning's, you'd have done better not to call. I almost fainted when they told me about the break-in. Great damage. You have no idea how great. And it's all your fault. . . ."

"Mine?"

"That's right. But let's put that aside for the moment.

What news do you have? Did you find out something about Jelena?"

"Yes . . . something interesting."

She waited for me to continue, but when I didn't she said impatiently, "Let's hear it."

"It's not for the telephone. Could we meet somewhere?"

She was about to object, but fell silent. Her encounter with Commissioner Milenković had clearly left an impression.

"I hope you're not thinking of that awful teashop."

"No. You choose the place."

It took her some time to decide.

"Café Mocha. On the corner . . ."

"I know where it is. When can you be there?"

"What time is it now?"

I looked at the corner of the computer screen.

"Eleven eighteen."

"Already? I'll be there at twelve thirty."

"Fine. See you then." I turned off my cellphone and put it back in my jacket pocket.

If I hadn't been counting on Miss Aksentijević's assistance, I would have been tempted to ask why she needed more than an hour to reach Café Mocha which, as I saw from her business card, was in her neighborhood. Fair enough, she was still in bed, but did she really need so much time to get ready after learning that I had news about her client? I supposed, however, it wouldn't be wise to annoy her further with such questions. And perhaps she could not get ready any faster in the morning after all, regardless of the urgency.

○ 20 ○

THIS WAS A CHANCE to look at the pictures of Miss Jakovljević's apartment and to try and sort out my thoughts without being disturbed. I had not had time

to catch my breath properly since everything had started the night before. Events had closed in on each other
just like in a detective story. Before opening the photograph file, I called Inspector Prokopović. We were
having a quiet Saturday morning so I did not have to
be in the duty room. I told him I was still working on
the break-in and would be going out in about half an
hour on a case-related job. I did not expect to be very
long. If something urgent came up, I could be reached
on my cell.

A slide show of scattered books began on the monitor. Something tightened in my chest just as it had that
morning when I'd been there in person. Only someone without the slightest respect for books would do
something like that. I could just imagine some vandal
snatching books off the shelves, riffling through them
and then throwing them all over the place, but why
were they doing it? And this was by no means the only
mysterious aspect of the break-in.

The ransacking clearly seemed to have some connection with Miss Jakovljević's disappearance, but this did
not necessarily have to be true. It might have been an
ordinary robbery. This assumption, being the simplest,
was not to be disregarded. Commissioner Milenković
was right, of course. Occam's razor could not be applied in every situation, but it must always be taken
into account. In an inspector's line of work it was advis-
able to be wary of accidents and coincidences, but they
should not be ruled out completely.

Everything, for example, could have taken place like
this: not suspecting what had happened in the apartment last evening, some burglar decided to break into
it last night. Even if they were watching the apartment,
they could easily have missed the two occasions when
I briefly turned on the lights. The windows were not
lit up for the most part, leading to the conclusion that
there was no one inside. They waited until the middle

of the night, entered the building without being seen and broke into the apartment. They would have been unpleasantly surprised to find the door locked from the inside, but Inspector Vesić had removed that obstacle.

Up to this point everything seemed plausible, but now the trouble began.

First of all, what plunder was the burglar hoping for? It would not have been hard to find out that a wealthy woman writer lived there, but did they expect her to keep money in her apartment? And what writer would keep it in a book? That would be a sacrilege. I had only been joking with Inspector Kostić when I said writers considered something safest when they hid it in a book.

The same thing was true of valuables, although they would not fit unless the book had been violated like in some third-rate spy movie by hollowing out the middle to make a repository. Such a cliché, however, would be the last resort of a detective story writer.

Indeed, the burglar did not have to be aware of these writerly taboos, but on the other hand, robberies like that are not undertaken without preparation. Break-ins are only made when plunder is assured. And if, perhaps, they had not been counting on money and valuables, what would they be looking for in the books?

As far as I could tell from the pictures, nothing else had been touched. The paintings had not been taken down, for example, in search of a hidden safe. Everything in the kitchen seemed in place. There was nothing to search in the bathroom. Of the items with any value, the computer could have been taken, but the burglar had shown no interest.

Then there was the noise that throwing the books must have made. Even burglars who don't care about leaving a trail behind them are always quiet, because noise gives them away the easiest. What was even more inexplicable about the noise was the fact that the neighbors in the apartment below had not heard a thing.

And there was no way to check whether the alleged painter Teodosijević had heard anything.

By all accounts, the idea of an ordinary break-in, although the simplest, had to be rejected. Something more complicated was going on. And the false Teodosijević was certainly involved.

Everything about him was a question mark. Who was he, anyway? Was he really blind? Why had he gone into the apartment of the real Teodosijević? Why had he called me back under the pretext that someone was in Miss Jakovljević's apartment? What did he actually know about her? Was he the one who drew my picture? If he was, when had he done it and why? Was he the one who broke into the apartment next door after I left, since it was no longer locked from the inside? What had he been looking for in the books? How could he have thrown them like that? How had he done it without being heard? Had he found what he was looking for? And finally—how had he disappeared from a building that was under Agency surveillance?

I was already well along with my examination of the pictures when something finally caught my eye. If I hadn't been deep in thought, I probably would have noted it earlier. Actually, I should have done so during my two visits to apartment number 19 the night before, but my attention had been directed at something else.

The pictures showed the books up close so I was able to read their titles. The person writing detective novels under the pseudonym Jelena Jakovljević had a discriminating taste in literature. There wasn't a single work that would be out of place in my own library. Furthermore, they were all hardback editions, some even leather bound. This seemed to confirm the internet conjecture that the real author came from the world of highbrow literature.

The fifty-some photographs ended with two extremely white ones that Inspector Kostić had taken in the bathroom. The first was taken from the door with the curtain pulled over the bathtub. In the second one the curtain was pulled aside; all that disturbed the uniformity of the bathtub was a small yellow object at the bottom, zoom-magnified. Who knew what had led the photographer to single out the rubber ducky in this way.

I reached for the mouse and closed the window with the pictures, then moved the cursor to the lower left-hand corner and turned off the computer. I pushed the button to turn off the monitor and had already started to get up from my desk when a sudden thought made me sit down again. It seemed to come out of the blue. Certainly nothing in the photographs had instigated it.

I wondered: could the man I had met as the painter Teodosijević, whose true identity I still did not know, be hiding behind the pseudonym Jelena Jakovljević?

At first glance, this assumption had a large drawback. It contradicted what Miss Aksentijević had said. She had presented her client as a woman and there was no reason to deceive the inspector she expected to track her down as soon as possible.

Or perhaps there was a reason. . . .

I felt a tingling sensation at the top of my spine. What if everything from the very beginning had been a performance intended to deceive the inspector? Not just any inspector, of course, but one who could be perfectly used in an original ad campaign for Jelena Jakovljević's new novel, *Find Me*.

I should have seen through them the night before as soon as the would-be painter started that twisted story about the Grand Manuscript, but fatigue seemed to have already taken its toll. Plus, I could not imagine that someone would be bold enough to try and manipulate me. But why not? As I had recently learned, lots of money was at stake and in such cases few holds are barred.

It was hard to think of better publicity for a new thriller than the writer's mysterious disappearance just after she had finished it, with the inspector trying to find her the same one who had already conducted an extremely unusual literary investigation—a case that, at least officially, had not been solved because neither the regular nor the secret police would accept an increase in the number of realities, so everything had been put *ad acta*. The Grand Manuscript had been concocted to tie into the inspector's case of the "Last Book".

The tangle of knots surrounding the false Teodosijević suddenly started to loosen. He was, of course, in collusion with his agent, Miss Aksentijević. It could not be any other way. Both of them had proven skillful actors and had succeeded in deluding me. Her anxiousness at the possibility that something had happened to Miss Jakovljević and her anger at not getting hold of the manuscript had been convincing, as was his performance as a blind painter, something obviously calculated to confuse me. The absence of the owner of the neighboring apartment had only played into his hands.

He had called me back, lying that someone was in Miss Jakovljević's apartment, just so he could mention the Grand Manuscript. He wanted to make me think that something extraordinary was happening again. He had probably commissioned my portrait from someone. The drawing was intended to confirm my connection to the case.

After I left, he had gone back into his apartment and ransacked it to make it look like someone had broken in for mysterious reasons. There was no need to make any noise if Miss Aksentijević helped him. The books gave the impression of having been tossed about, but they could have been quietly positioned that way. Lastly, someone who was familiar with the building could have left it at night without being seen, even with the Agency keeping an eye on it, just as they could have stayed hidden somewhere inside.

Indeed, all that had to be proven was the initial

premise that the detective story writer was an unknown person who had posed as a blind painter, but the consequences were so elegantly simple they seemed made to measure for Occam. Even so, I had to stifle the excitement that came over me. There were still several questions awaiting answers.

For example, how could they be certain that I would be the one to come last night? It could have been some other inspector. Even if they found out that I was on duty, it was still no guarantee that I would come and not the other person on duty with me.

Then, how had they managed to lock the door from the inside without being inside? According to Inspector Vesić it was impossible, at least for that type of lock, and he was the greatest expert around.

Then, why had Miss Aksentijević given Commissioner Milenković such a good description of her client? Shouldn't she have kept his identity hidden? Had she been frightened, not having counted on the National Security Agency getting involved in the whole thing? Or had she realized there was no sense in describing him otherwise since I had seen him too, and the other tenants in the building must have seen him from time to time? And what if that was not his real appearance? What if he had been in disguise last night?

Finally, there was the greatest enigma—two extremely unusual cellphones. If the publisher was ready to invest the wherewithal to promote his new edition, an explanation could be found for all the rest, but not for this gadget. I had taken to it so effortlessly, even though it was impossible in all respects. It worked without a SIM card and battery, it closely monitored me even when inside my pocket, and I received messages as though my unknown collocutor was writing them instantaneously.

Just as this thought crossed my mind, vibrations started in my pocket again.

I HESITATED JUST A moment and then took out the cellphone. Did it have another impossible characteristic—the ability to be invisible to Commissioner Milenković? The person I was exchanging SMS messages with had said *"Let me worry about that. . . ."* and I was convinced she was Jelena Jakovljević. If she had underestimated the commissioner, I would be in double trouble. I would have to explain why I had kept this other telephone secret, and he would certainly take it away from me. I didn't want to break off contact with this mysterious individual, of course, and I felt she was equally anxious to stay in contact with me. And I supposed she knew what she was doing when she wrote that. . . .

Before I opened the new message, I glanced up at the ceiling. It seemed probable that the hidden camera was up there somewhere, although that did not have to be true. The smile trembling on my lips was an oxymoronic combination of apology for being disloyal to our cooperation and defiance for staying outside the National Security Agency's field of vision, as I hoped. This hope would be in vain if the service phone in the inside pocket of my jacket started ringing in a few moments. I waited briefly, but when no sound disturbed the silence in my office, I pushed the button on the black phone's keypad to open messages.

I expected another derisive remark—this had already become a disagreeable habit of my unknown collocutor—but for the first time there was no text. I looked in bewilderment at the last picture I had received from Inspector Kostić: the yellow ducky parading on the bottom of the bathtub.

The first thing I should have wondered, of course, was how the sender had got hold of this picture. Kostić had no reason to send the on-site investigation photographs to anyone else, and it was impossible for someone from the outside to enter the closed police communications system and get them that way. But this issue seemed less important than another one. Why had I been sent this of all pictures? Most likely it had not been chosen at random just to show me that our communications system was not as impenetrable at it seemed.

I was tempted to reply with a message containing just a question mark, but then thought better of it. This was clearly some sort of riddle and a question mark would mean that I was unable to solve it and was asking for help. My pride would not let me. Also, there was no time for a new chat session. These would have been shorter if I could master the skill of instantaneous texting, but unfortunately I was far from it. And it was already seven minutes after twelve, as I saw on the cell's screen before returning the phone to my pants pocket.

I had spent more time than I realized looking through the photographs and would have to hurry to get to Café Mocha before twelve-thirty. Even though it was Saturday, traffic was doubtless lively by now and the café was in a different part of town.

As I drove the car out of the police headquarters underground garage, I suddenly found myself in a predicament. The natural thing would be to take the shortest route, but I would have preferred a more roundabout way even if it meant being a little late, just so I could avoid a street that I had not taken for a year and a half.

I lingered at the garage exit trying to make up my mind until another car emerged. The flashing high beams forced me to decide. You can't run away from the past by refusing to face it.

Even though neither of the two places that tied my memories to that street still existed, I felt a thrill when I turned onto it. I knew what stores had replaced the old ones. The Mandarin Teashop was now the Lucky Hand second-hand shop. As I passed by, I saw it was closed. It was nondescript from the outside, like most such stores, I supposed.

The Oriental teashop proprietor and his twins had disappeared without a trace as soon as the "Last Book" case had ended. Even though I tried, I had not succeeded in finding out what happened to them. Had they fled somewhere to elude the unpleasant investigation or was the National Security Agency behind their disappearance? Commissioner Milenković could have told me, but he had no reason to do me any favors. Besides, last night was the first time I had seen him since that case.

I had not been able to dodge the investigation, but it had been short and without consequences, contrary to my expectations. I told them what I knew without concealing anything or presenting things in a different light. My story was duly noted with no astonishment as though the case, while indeed unusual, was certainly not outlandish. Ultimately, all I had to do was pledge that I would never reveal anything about the Last Book. I continued doing my job as though nothing had happened. It seemed that my colleagues had been ordered to stifle their curiosity. No one tried to ferret anything out about the case.

A Fragrance high-end cosmetics chain store now stood in place of the Papyrus Bookstore. It was all metal and glass, illuminated by bright lights even in the middle of the day. I slowed down a little as I passed by. I saw a crowd of customers through the large display window but not a single armchair. No one had any reason to stay there longer than they needed to buy a quick body beautification product. Slow beautification of the soul definitely did not go along with cosmetic glamour.

Vera had closed the bookstore just two weeks after the "Last Book" case was brought to a conclusion. She had tried briefly to run it herself, but it was too much responsibility for one person. She hired an assistant, but that hadn't worked either. She missed Olga in many respects. Furthermore, the bookstore had become a hangout for annoying curiosity seekers. It was not books that interested most visitors but recent events; their mysteriousness had only increased with the official hush-up and unrelenting articles in the tabloids. Even organized tourist groups had started coming.

The bookstore was supposed to be closed only temporarily until the dust settled, but weeks passed and Vera showed no desire to go back to selling books. When the Fragrance chain made an offer to buy the store, she accepted it without a second thought. The offer had indeed been high, probably owing to the popularity of the location. She kept the books and furnishings in order to open a new bookstore somewhere else. At least that had been her intention.

We kept on seeing each other, but only at her place. She never came to mine. I invited her, of course, until I realized where the problem lay. She had an aversion to my study. It was identical to the other study from the other reality where the novel *The Last Book* had been written. And the cost of writing that novel had been the death of six people in our reality.

I too had trouble accepting the existence of two realities, but it helped that they were no longer crossed. I could pretend that ours was the only one. It was harder for Vera. Whenever she opened her eyes she saw a reminder from the other reality—colors. That weighed her down the most. *The Last Book*'s writer had made amends, but the gift she received had become a mark of culpability. She had not been able to refuse it and that seemed to make her an accomplice in six-fold murder. She would gladly have become color blind again if that would bring back the dead. Or at least one of them—Olga.

By tacit agreement we avoided talking about it. That had seemed best. Soon, unfortunately, we stopped talking about almost anything. Vera withdrew further and further into silence and I could not find a way to break through her shell. I might have succeeded if I'd spent more time with her, but a police inspector's job devours time relentlessly. . . .

On the thirty-seventh day after the "Last Book" case was closed, I received a brief, vague SMS from Vera. *"I'm leaving. Don't look for me. I'll be in touch."* Of course I didn't listen to her. I used every means I had at my disposal as an inspector to find her, but the earth seemed to have swallowed her up.

When it was clear that I would not succeed, in my despair I was tempted to turn to Commissioner Milenković for help. If anyone could track her down, it was the National Security Agency. But I didn't do it. Not because I doubted that the commissioner would be willing to help, as I had not helped him in the case that became a stain on his service's otherwise spotless history. I held back because I suspected that Vera would not forgive me for finding her through the Agency. She would have considered it my ultimate betrayal.

And so all I could do was put my trust in the promise from the last sentence of Vera's message. A year and a half had passed since she'd disappeared, however, and she still had not gotten in touch. There was no sense in waiting any longer. The time had come to surrender one chapter of my life to the past. There was no reason to avoid this street anymore.

I stepped on the gas so I would not be late at Café Mocha.

∽ 22 ∾

I WAS IN FRONT of Café Mocha a little before twelve-thirty and then lost ten minutes parking. I cruised around looking for a free spot, but they were all taken. In the end I left the car in an unauthorized place. I used this privilege reluctantly because it singled me out. An illegally parked car without a ticket under the windshield wipers told someone with an attentive eye that the police were nearby. Perhaps I should have a ticket ready for such occasions. Funny that I hadn't thought of it before.

The crowd inside the café reflected the one in front of it. Nice weather on a Saturday had lured people out of their homes. I saw at a glance that all the tables were taken and so were the stools at the bar. Moving a little to the side so as not to block the entrance, I began searching for Miss Aksentijević in the large room. But she had not yet arrived.

I raised the left sleeve of my jacket a fraction. Twenty to one. She would probably get here at any moment, and then what? We had nowhere to sit and would have to go somewhere else. Better to wait outside in the sun, I thought. Just as I began to turn toward the exit, a young couple got up from a round table nearby.

He was burly with short hair, wearing sports clothes, and had a striking tattoo on his left earlobe. She was small and plump with straight, long, dark hair, flashily dressed. There was a tiny mole on the tip of her nose. They were holding hands. As they passed by, the girl smiled at me.

"For you, Inspector," she said softly, motioning her head toward the table.

They did not turn around to see my reaction. I waited for them to go out and then sat on the closest chair. Commissioner Milenković had clearly taken our cooperation seriously. I would have to find a way to repay him for this service. I looked around the café again, hoping to catch sight of him in a corner, but he wasn't there.

Then I noted five of his possible associates at two tables. Provided, of course, I was not wrong about the Agency bringing in fresh blood and its new members' informal dress and adornment code. If I was right, the commissioner had some reason to consider my upcoming meeting very important, judging by how many people he had deployed.

A waitress in a brown uniform soon came over. She put the previous customers' barely touched soft drinks on a tray and asked me what I wanted. I hesitated briefly over whether to wait for Miss Aksentijević before ordering, and then asked for a cappuccino. There had been no chance for a cup of coffee since morning, and Café Mocha was filled with fragrant caffeine.

The cappuccino seemed to have an enlightening effect on me. The very first sip brought a thought that made me wonder for the second time that morning why it had not occurred to me before. I sat there stock-still for several moments, holding the cup to my mouth.

I was there to coax Miss Aksentijević into describing the person who wrote under the pseudonym Jelena Jakovljević. I did not expect her to capitulate just like that because she had no reason to be accommodating. I could warn her about refusing to cooperate with the police, but even if I frightened her in that way, I was not certain to get what I wanted. This might not happen even if I promised in return to give her what she coveted, although I didn't have it—the manuscript of the novel *Find Me*.

If she was determined to hide the identity of her client, she could put me on the wrong track with a phony description. There would be no way to confirm what she said. Nevertheless, I had to try. The only thing I knew for sure about her was that she had seen the mysterious writer. I counted on being able to tell whether she was lying.

But what if she had to keep the description secret regardless of the cost, not to protect her client but so she wouldn't describe herself? It should have occurred to me first that she, and not the alleged painter Teodosijević, was Jelena Jakovljević. Everything that concerned him could apply even more to her.

With her in the main role an ingenious ad campaign for the new novel also stood behind it all and I was to have an important, although unwilling, bit part too. The false Teodosijević had been Miss Aksentijević's assistant in last night's performance that had been calculated to involve me in a sophisticated game. She had enticed me to the building, pretending to be a panic-stricken agent, and then the blind painter had come onstage, increasing the aura of mystery.

First he had persistently maintained that Miss Jakovljević was still in the apartment even after I had established that it was empty. Then when I came back because of the so-called break-in, he had passed off the story of the Grand Manuscript that was intended to convince me that the case was similar to the "Last Book". Finally, he had helped Miss Aksentijević quietly set the scene of disorder in the writer's apartment. That was the end of his role and he could disappear without a trace. This would have been all the easier if he'd been in disguise the night before, so Miss Aksentijević would have nothing to worry about when she described him in detail to Commissioner Milenković.

Search Publishers most likely did not know the agent was hiding behind the pseudonym, otherwise the information would have been leaked by now. The competition would have had no trouble finding someone to reveal the secret for the right sum. Part of Jelena Jakovljević's popularity lay in the enigma surrounding her identity. The publisher did not necessarily have to know it if Miss Aksentijević had authorized herself in her capacity as an agent to sign contracts with them.

Nevertheless, the premise that Miss Aksentijević was the detective story writer came up against the same unanswered questions as the premise about the man who pretended to be Teodosijević the painter. How could they be sure that I would come last night? How had they been able to lock the door from the inside without being inside? Where had they got a telephone that worked without a SIM card and battery?

I was really interested to hear what Miss Aksentijević had to say about these riddles. The best thing would be to tell her straight out, as soon as she sat down, that I had found Miss Jakovljević. She would be unprepared for such a move. If she was the one, it would show on her face.

I finished my cappuccino, put down the cup and looked at my watch again. Seven minutes to one. I sighed. Some writers had a bad reputation for their easy-going attitude toward time, but I had imagined that agents were more responsible. Did she need an hour and a half to get ready? And after I'd said I had news for her?

A sudden thought cut into my meditations. What if she had sensed I was on to her and decided not to come? No, that was impossible. Nothing I'd said could have led her to that conclusion. After all, when we'd talked I hadn't suspect her at all. The possibility had just crossed my mind there in the café.

I took out my service phone and called the last number again. After a brief silence a mechanical female voice said the person who had been called was unavailable at the moment. I put the phone back in my pocket. I sat there a while longer, deep in thought, and then opened the brown menu to see how much a cappuccino cost. I put some money next to the saucer and got up. There was no reason to keep waiting.

I left the Café Mocha with the eerie feeling that eyes were drilling holes in my back. I squinted in the bright sunlight and then headed for my car. Just before reaching it I stopped and took out Miss Aksentijević's business card to check the address. I was sure she would not be at home, but why not try since I was already in the neighborhood?

The old four-story building somewhat farther down

the street had large balconies and a steep roof. My eyes slid down the row of names on the intercom next to the glass front door. I would have found what I was looking for right away if I had started at the bottom. The next-to-last name at number 11 said "Ljubica Aksentijević, literary agent".

I pushed the gray button. The reply was almost instantaneous, as though someone had been standing next to the intercom at the other end.

"Please come in, Inspector Lukić."

I recognized the young female voice immediately, although I had only heard it once before.

꙰ 23 ꙰

As I CLIMBED TO the fourth floor, I remembered Miss Aksentijević complaining the night before that she was not in shape because she smoked. It must have been hard living on the top floor of a building without an elevator where the stairs were so steep. Even I was a bit out of breath.

The girl with a mole on the tip of her nose was standing at the door to apartment 11.

"Fifty-four stairs," she said with a smile.

"Good count," I agreed gloomily.

"I only counted to the second floor. Then I multiplied by three."

"You shouldn't always depend on stairs being the way you expect them to be."

"I intended to double check on the way down." Her smile broadened. "Now I don't have to."

She opened the door all the way and closed it after I entered. "This way," she said, leading me toward the other end of the short hall.

The scene awaiting me in the study did not affect me as much as the one that morning because the proportions were smaller. Of the two narrow shelves, the one with books had been almost emptied, while the other one full of large black file folders was untouched. The contents of the four desk drawers had joined the fifty-some books scattered on the floor. The drawers had clearly been tossed after being emptied because two of them lay there in pieces.

The young man with the tattooed earlobe was crouched down by one of them. He was wearing white latex gloves, and a large black bag with equipment for collecting forensic samples was open next to him. From where I stood I could not see what he was examining, but I assumed from the pipette he was using around the bottom of the broken drawer that there was a bloodstain there. The girl who had greeted me put on gloves too and joined him.

The woman photographer I had already met was taking pictures of the desk, where everything was in disorder as well. The keyboard was awry, the monitor upside down, the receiver was off the telephone hook, felt-tip pens and paper clips were scattered all about, a vase of flowers had been knocked over next to the edge, and yellow juice had spilled from a tall glass. The girl raised her head briefly toward me and smiled. I replied with a short nod.

"We've started seeing more of each other, Inspector Lukić," came the voice of Commissioner Milenković from behind my back.

I moved aside to let him into the study from the hall. He was holding the upper edge of a steaming plastic cup between his left fingers, a tea bag string hanging over the top.

"That's in the spirit of two-way cooperation."

"Ah, yes, cooperation. It almost slipped my mind. All right, shall we cooperate a little more?"

"Excuse me?"

"You know, like last time. First one asks a question and then the other."

"All right."

"I'm listening."

I thought for a moment. "When did you enter the apartment?"

"At 12:35. While you were looking for a place to park."

"Did you have a reason?"

"We wanted to see why Miss Aksentijević was not on her way to meet you. First we called her cell, but it had been turned off. . . ."

"What would you have done if she had answered?" I said, interrupting him. "Reprimand her for being late?"

He raised his eyes over the plastic cup as he started blowing into it.

"If she had answered, we would have excused ourselves for dialing the wrong number. And if she had answered the intercom that we then rang, we would not have said anything, leaving her to believe it was a childish prank. But since there was no answer, we entered the apartment."

"Did you have the building under surveillance?"

"Of course. No one went in or out after 11:47."

"I assume you didn't find her here . . . injured?" I nodded toward the young man and girl who were still examining the broken drawer.

"No, we didn't. There was no one in the locked apartment. We still don't know if that is her blood."

"It looks like we now have a kidnapping along with a break-in."

He took a cautious sip of tea from the cup. "Yes, that's what it looks like. Although they don't really go together. Burglars mostly try to avoid the people they burgle. If their paths do cross, they might even resort to murder, but not kidnapping."

"Do you mean to say that the ransacking is fake? A front for kidnapping?"

"It might be."

"Even if that's what happened, how could the kidnappers get out without being seen by your surveillance?"

"You're asking me a lot, Inspector Lukić. I still don't have all the answers. But another question plagues me more than that one right now. What is the connection between the kidnapping and your meeting with Miss Aksentijević?"

"Why would those two events be connected?"

"Because it would be naive to assume that their chronological concurrence was accidental. Kidnappings don't happen in the middle of the day under the National Security Agency's nose unless they are absolutely necessary. For example, to make sure that two people don't see each other. Who knew about your meeting?"

"No one. Except you, of course."

"You're certain you didn't tell anyone?"

"You would know if I had. You keep an eye on me all the time. In the spirit of two-way cooperation."

"You can't keep your eye on someone all the time. Particularly if they know about it. And if they have a reason to hide something. In the spirit of two-way cooperation."

We looked at each other in silence for several moments. I broke the silence first.

"No one else knew about the meeting. I told Inspector Prokopović, who is on duty with me today, that I would be going out to do something for the case I was working on, but didn't give him any details."

"Someone found out anyway."

"How?"

Commissioner Milenković slowly took another sip of tea.

"Maybe they tapped your conversation with Miss Aksentijević," he said in a lower voice.

"You can't tap a police service phone."

"Every telephone can be tapped. All you need is the proper equipment. And I know who has that equipment. The problem is that no one used it. I checked."

"So how could someone have tapped me?"

"That's another question I can't answer. There are too many of them already. Ever since that impossible cellphone turned up last night my life has become very complicated."

I smiled in commiseration. "Mine too, if it helps any."

He tried to return my smile, but all he managed was a grimace.

"What was the news you wanted to tell Miss Aksentijević?"

"There was no news."

"Inspector Lukić!" he said in a raised voice, looking at me reproachfully. "We're cooperating, remember?"

"How could I forget? I really didn't have anything to tell her. It was just an excuse to get together."

"As far as I remember, she's not exactly your type."

The girl, who was now photographing the books and contents of the drawers on the floor, cleared her throat. The commissioner turned his head toward her briefly.

"She's not. I was interested in another woman. Miss Aksentijević is the only one who can tell me what Miss Jelena Jakovljević looks like."

"Oh, yes. The mysterious Miss Jakovljević. You were surprised when you discovered it was a pseudonym, weren't you?"

"Was my surprise so obvious?"

"Not at all, but I've become skilled at detecting the unobvious. By the way, that's not her biggest surprise."

"There's an even bigger one?"

"Yes, but you won't find anything about it on the internet. It's a highly guarded secret. I had no idea that publishers were such tough nuts to crack. Even I had to use some elbow grease to get hold of it at Search."

"You found out her identity?"

Commissioner Milenković took another sip from the plastic cup. The tea was no longer steaming.

"Which of the eight identities were you thinking of?"

I stared at him for several moments in silence.

"Eight?" I repeated at last.

"Yes. It's a collective identity. As someone well-versed in literature, you certainly know about that. But for an ignoramus like me, it was completely new."

"You mean to say that several writers are hiding behind the pseudonym Jelena Jakovljević?"

"Eight. Every novel written under that name came from the pen of a different author."

"Do you know who they are?"

"I do, but I have to keep it to myself. It is highly confidential business information. The Agency would be in hot water if it was leaked."

"All right, all right. Those eight don't interest me, but the ninth one does. Did you find out who wrote the new novel that will be published under the pseudonym Jelena Jakovljević?"

"No, unfortunately. We would have found that out too, but not even they know. The author's anonymity was a key item in the contract this time. It seems that the writer of the ninth novel is a really great name in literature. They suspect two authors that even I have heard of." He paused for a moment. "If you ask me, it's pure hypocrisy. The kingpins from highbrow literature will do their best to hide any involvement with detective novels, but won't be the least bit appalled by the big money that goes along with them. I never imagined that books about our profession were so well paid. It's much more profitable to write about detectives than to be one."

I smiled. "It's still not too late to change your profession."

"That's not for me. I'm better at solving cases than making them up. All right, now it's back to work. We've had enough cooperation this time. We'll have occasion, I hope, to see each other again soon."

I nodded my head and the inspector's two female associates replied in kind. I was already in the hall when the commissioner's voice stopped me.

"I forgot to ask, Inspector Lukić." He raised his plastic cup. "Are you still fond of tea?"

I hesitated a moment before answering. "I am."

"It's an excellent drink. I myself have become an enthusiast. Sometimes it seems to have a miraculous effect."

～ 24 ～

I TOOK THE STEEP stairs down from the fourth floor. Everything that Commissioner Milenković had just told me was consistent with my assumption that Miss Aksentijević was the ninth writer to use the pseudonym Jelena Jakovljević. This would have been all the easier to pull off if she did not have to tell Search whom she was representing. The publishers must have had great confidence in her if they'd agreed to such an unusual arrangement—not knowing whose work they were publishing. This probably came from her being the agent of the previous eight writers too.

This would also explain the eight paintings in the small room of apartment 19 on Oak Street. Otherwise it would make no sense for the author of the ninth novel to have the framed covers of the earlier works by other writers. Only one person had a reason: the only real person who connected all the books. The same agent.

Over time she had probably given her role in the success of the detective series too much credit and thought it was time finally to have a go as Jelena Jakovljević. She knew, however, that she would never be accepted as the author, so she concocted the story of a great writer who insisted on remaining anonymous, even to the publisher.

Search had no reason to suspect anything. It suited them to get a top literary name even if it was only under such conditions. And what was more fitting for a top name than the same kind of ad campaign—full of mystery, just like Jelena Jakovljević's books? Miss Aksentijević had certainly been willing to take part in it.

It was not hard to establish why her alleged kidnapping had come about. Our meeting had nothing to do with it. Search Publishers had called to tell her about the visit of a National Security Agency commissioner and she was afraid they might soon come to see her again to inquire about the identity of the person writing the ninth novel. This would let the cat out of the bag.

She had staged the ransacking and then left the apartment. She might still be in the building or might have left it without being seen, like the phony painter Teodosijević, in the morning. She had taken care to damage her apartment as little as possible. Books were scattered so they resembled the break-in in the other apartment, but also because they could be easily put back in place. The same was true of the contents of the drawers, and even the disorder on the desk was not really very great.

The blood would probably turn out to be hers, but it could have come from a harmless little cut, not a serious injury. The files, however, had not been touched. If someone had really been searching for something well hidden in her apartment, they would have looked there first. And putting the files back in order would have taken the longest time.

How wise was Commissioner Milenković to all of this? Not very, I'd say, but that might just be appearances. The fact that we were now cooperating meant nothing. He would never tell me everything he knew and it was always better to assume that he knew more rather than less. This was confirmed by his allusion to tea at the end of the conversation.

He had seemed sincerely worried about the possibility of someone completely unknown to him being able to tap police cellphones. If the assumption about Miss Aksentijević being the ninth Jelena Jakovljević was true, he could rest at ease. The Agency had no competition. No one else had tapped me. There had been no need.

All I could do was hope to find an elegant solution for what worried me too. But I was still not one step closer to answering those three questions: how could whoever had devised this be certain that I would be the one to appear last night; how could they lock an apartment from the inside without being inside; and where did that impossible telephone come from?

Without those answers my assumption was not worth much, so the danger still loomed that someone was tapping my service telephone. I would have to be careful when I used it, just in case.

I left the four-story building and headed for my car, but stopped after only three steps and quickly went back. I tried to open the door, but it was already too late. I remained there several moments staring through the glass at the staircase, then headed for my car once again. I could have rung the bell at apartment 11 and asked to be let back into the building, but what explanation could I offer? That I wanted to count the stairs again because the automatic counter inside me had reached only fifty-two as I walked down, deep in thought? They would think I had lost my mind, and nothing more convincing occurred to me.

As I walked down the sunny street, I wondered how to proceed now that Miss Aksentijević had decided that the safest thing for her was to disappear. I could look for the answers to my questions at Search Publishers. If

I was not mistaken, that's where the intricate and expense ad campaign for *Find Me* had been worked out.

That would have to wait until Monday. I doubted I would find anyone in their offices over the weekend, particularly after the Agency's unexpected visit. Commissioner Milenković had ways to convince publishers to get together on a Saturday morning so he could question them, but I was just an ordinary police inspector. Indeed, I could have tried something through Miss Timotijević, but I had no reason to hurry. On the contrary. If I had indeed been forced into a bit part in this show, I didn't have actually to identify with it.

I was already close to my car when ringing reverberated from my jacket pocket. It took a few moments to realize it was my private cell. The last time I'd heard it was before this case began. I took it out and looked at the screen. I didn't recognize the number.

"Hello?"

"Inspector Dejan Lukić?"

"Yes."

"Hello, Inspector. Jelisaveta Šumanović from the *Evening Courier* speaking. Would you give us a statement?"

"Where did you get my private phone number?" I replied with a question.

"You know that we never disclose our source of information."

"And you know that the police spokesperson is the only one authorized to make statements."

The line was briefly silent.

"You won't believe me if I tell you."

"It's that unbelievable?"

"It's that stupid. You'll think I have absolutely no imagination for not coming up with something cleverer."

"I would never think that a lady had absolutely no imagination."

"I'll take that as a compliment."

"You would be correct."

"I was given your number in an email," she said after another brief pause.

"Who sent it?"

"It was anonymous."

"Was there anything else in the email besides my cellphone number?"

"Yes. Shall I read it to you?"

"Please do."

"Call Inspector Dejan Lukić and ask him what he has to say about last night's break-in at writer Jelena Jakovljević's apartment."

"I have nothing to add to what you will get in the regular police bulletin at two o'clock. A routine break-in case."

The journalist cleared her throat.

"Excuse me. There's more in the email."

"Let's hear it."

"If the inspector says it is a routine break-in, ask him what the door of an empty apartment locked from the inside has to do with it."

Now I was silent for a moment.

"Do you expect me to believe it really says that?"

"Word for word. If you want, I can forward the email to you."

"I think it would be best to say goodbye. Being without imagination is not good, but overdoing it is even worse."

"Please don't hang up. Let me at least read you the end, it's the most imaginative part. Aren't you interested?"

I hesitated a moment.

"I'm listening."

"And ask him about the telephone that works without a SIM card and battery."

She stopped, clearly waiting for me to say something.

"Is that the end now?" I asked.

"No. There's one more sentence. Finally, ask him about the connection between the break-in and the 'Last Book' case."

When I did not say anything, the journalist spoke up again.

"Would you care to answer these questions, Inspector Lukić? Was the door really locked from the inside? What kind of cellphone works without a SIM card and battery? Is the 'Last Book' case being reopened?"

"I do not answer questions from anonymous messages, but I believe you."

"What do you believe?"

"That you really did receive an email with the contents you read to me. I even know who sent it."

"Who?"

"Someone who was convinced you would take the bait. That you would report on all of this."

"Maybe I wouldn't if you told me a bit more. Alluding to some sort of bait is not really enough. . . ."

"I told you as much as I could, Mrs. Šumanović."

"Miss . . ."

"Miss, excuse me. It should be enough for an imaginative lady. Goodbye."

I ended the call and sighed. I should have expected the dust being raised around *Find Me* to start in a tabloid like the *Evening Courier*. Miss Šumanović would certainly not be deterred by my vague warning and flattery. What she had been offered was inflammatory enough for her to take no consideration of what I thought. The publisher had immediately pulled out the three strongest trump cards that were still a puzzle to me.

I put the phone back in my jacket pocket and then took out my car key. I turned off the alarm and sat behind the wheel. I had to do a bit of maneuvering to get out because in the meantime my space had been narrowed by another illegally parked car.

The ringing started just as I entered Chestnut Boulevard. I thought it was the phone in my pants pocket ringing for the first time because the ring tone differed from my private and service phones. I almost lost control of the car when I realized that the ringing was coming from the back seat.

∾ 25 ∽

HOLDING THE STEERING WHEEL firmly, I glanced over my shoulder and saw a cellphone on the seat behind me. It was the same gray color as the seat cover. I quickly faced front again and barely suppressed the urge to grab the phone to stop the piercing sound as it intensified. If I had tried, however, I probably would have caused an accident. Traffic around me was lively and the cell was hard to reach.

I started looking for a place to stop and soon realized it would not be easy. I could not give in to psychosis, however, and do something rash. The initial surprise had already subsided so I was able to think more clearly. There was actually no reason for haste.

Indeed, why should I rush to answer the phone, apart from the ringing that was grating on my nerves? Even if it stopped ringing, there would be a trace of the missed call's number. And if there wasn't, the person would call again. They certainly had not taken the trouble to leave the phone in a police inspector's official car just to give up after the first attempt to reach him failed.

I couldn't imagine how they had pulled it off. Not only was the car alarm on, but Commissioner Milenković's people must have been keeping an eye on the whole stretch of street from Café Mocha to Miss Aksentijević's apartment, including my car. That was customary procedure even for ordinary police during an operation. The surroundings are always monitored, just in case. And I could see no reason for the commissioner not to inform me that someone was fooling around my car or not to prevent it.

A free spot suddenly appeared. My abrupt braking without a signal caused a chain of squealing tires, honking and angry shouts behind me. I had to unbuckle my seat belt and get up off my seat in order to reach the cellphone that was ringing without letup, but at least the unpleasant sound had stopped getting louder.

I did not recognize the number on the screen. I took a look at the gray phone before answering. From the outside it appeared to be a simple model.

"Hello," I said.

"Hello, Inspector Lukić," replied a young female voice. "Thank you for answering."

"Who are you?"

"Someone who has a good reason to talk to you."

"Is this the simplest way for us to talk?"

"No, but simpler ways are not reliable. Our conversation needs to be confidential."

"And that justifies breaking into a police car? Are you aware that it is a serious offence?"

"Are there any traces of a break-in? Did the alarm go off?"

"The phone did not appear on the back seat all by itself."

"Why don't you ask the National Security Agency how the telephone got there? They had your car under surveillance and they videoed it the whole time too."

I fell silent for a few moments.

"What do you want to talk about?"

"About the novel *Find Me*. We are interested in the file of the final manuscript."

"Why don't you talk to the publishers? They own it."

"Yes, but they don't have it. They didn't get it from the author."

"Then see with the author."

"Do you know where she is?"

"No, I don't. And I don't know why you called me about it, either."

"Because we think you might have the file."

"Me? How could I have the file?"

"You were alone in Miss Jakovljević's apartment twice last night, right?"

"You are well informed."

"Even better than you think. That was your chance to get hold of it."

"I was looking for Miss Jakovljević, not some manuscript."

"That still doesn't mean you didn't take it."

"Why on earth would I do that?"

"Because you knew how much it was worth."

"All I knew was that she received a large advance from the publisher. But what kind of motive would that be for taking it?"

"I wasn't thinking of that kind of worth."

"What kind were you thinking of?"

A hint of impatience appeared in the otherwise composed voice.

"Let's not waste valuable time needlessly, Inspector Lukić. You know perfectly well what worth I have in mind. We are talking about the Grand Manuscript."

"Oh, that. The first time I heard about the Grand Manuscript was not until after my second visit to Miss Jakovljević's apartment last night."

"You don't expect us to believe that, do you?"

"Believe whatever you want. In any case, I don't have the file with the novel's manuscript. But even if I did, what would you want?"

"For you to give it to us, of course."

"Why would I give it to you? It doesn't belong to you."

"Because you would get the most from us. Far more than from the others."

"What others? There are no others."

"There were, but they bluffed you to get hold of the manuscript for free. Soon, however, you will be showered with offers. The Grand Manuscript is a very hot property."

"Trying to bribe a police inspector is a considerably more aggravated offence than breaking into his car."

"With what we'd give you, you could leave your poorly paid police inspector's job and spend the rest of your life in luxury."

"Something doesn't add up here."

"What?"

"If you really believe the story about the first person who reads the Grand Manuscript becoming immortal, then if I did have it why would I sell it and not use it myself? Nothing you offer me could be greater than immortality."

"We believe in the Grand Manuscript, but you don't. You think it's preposterous, so why not sell the file for a high price?"

"Even if I don't believe it, what would it cost me to read it first, just in case?"

"It would cost you dearly. Immortality does not mean an easy life forever. You can be immortal in hell too. And we would do our best to arrange a suitable never-ending hell. I heartily advise you not to open that file, let alone start to read it."

"Thank you for your advice. It's easy to accept because I have nothing to open. Let me repeat—I have never had possession of the file."

We sank into a brief silence.

"Too bad, Inspector Lukić. If you'd been reasonable, everything would have worked out to the advantage of us both. This way, we have no choice but to see for ourselves whether or not you've read the Grand Manuscript."

"How will you do that?"

"It's simple enough. If you've become immortal,

you'll have no trouble passing a test that mere mortals fail."

"Test?"

"Yes. We've already had one today. We suspected one other person of having read *Find Me*, but it turned out they hadn't. Unfortunately they did not survive. Such is the nature of the test."

"What person? What was the test?"

"You'll soon find out."

I sighed.

"How about cutting this show short? Things have really gone far enough. Tell your employers at Search not to string the police along like this. It's deplorable to abuse us like puppets in an ad campaign for Jelena Jakovljević's new book. Someone will be held criminally responsible."

My unknown collocutor suddenly seemed at a loss for words.

"What ad campaign are you talking about, Inspector?"

Just as I was about to reply, the phone in my jacket pocket started ringing.

"Wait a moment." I put the gray phone on the seat next to me and took out my service phone. "Hello," I said promptly without looking at who was calling.

"Inspector Lukić," said Inspector Prokopović, "we've received a report about a woman who was found in the elevator at 12 Oak Street. She seems to be dead. I just sent an on-site investigation team."

"I'm not far, I'll be there right away."

I put the service phone back in my pocket and then picked up the gray one.

"Hello?"

In return came the silence of a disconnected line.

∽ 26 ∾

I WAS MOMENTARILY UNCERTAIN what to do with the gray telephone, then put it in my left pants pocket. Never before had I had four cellphones on me. The next time one of them rang, it was unlikely I'd be able to tell which one it was right away. As I watched for a chance to pull out of my parking spot, glancing over my right shoulder, I wondered why they had left the little gray phone on the seat behind the driver and not, for example, in the glove box in front of the seat next to me where it would be better hidden.

In all probability, they had not wanted me to notice it too soon. The chances were much greater of my looking for something in the glove box than on the back seat. Although in plain sight, the cell behind me had blended like a chameleon with the seat cover. I'd had no reason to look on the back seat when I entered the car, but even if I had it would have been easy to overlook. If it hadn't rung, who knows how long it would have ridden around with me.

A sudden thought made me sit upright behind the wheel. Maybe the same thing applied to the past. I could not rule out the possibility that the cell had been in the car with me for some time, but had not caught my eye. They might have put it in earlier and not now while the car was under Agency surveillance. They would still have had to take care of the alarm, but that was an easier hurdle for someone determined to outsmart the police.

I looked over my shoulder again and realized it would be some time before I pulled out into the street. I didn't like to use the rotating light, but now I had no choice. I took it out of the glove box and put it on the roof. I had to turn on the siren too before I finally moved out.

I had the right of way, but it was hard to use it on

the congested boulevard. I was only able to drive faster when I turned off it. Then I didn't need the rotating light and siren anymore, so I turned them off.

The production concocted by Search was reaching its dénouement. The woman in the elevator who seemed to be dead would, of course, turn out to be alive. Publishers had indeed lost all sense of proportion in their ad campaigns, but no one would be bold enough to kill. I couldn't figure out who the alleged victim was, the one they suspected of reading *Find Me*. Who had had access to the manuscript? As far as I could tell, no one had seen it yet.

I reached the building at 12 Oak Street first. Traffic had clearly slowed down the on-site inspection team and Commissioner Milenković. There was no place to park, so I stopped at the entrance. A long-haired young man in worn-out jeans and a thin brick-colored sweatshirt was standing in front of the glass door. His running shoes were loosely laced.

"Hello, Inspector Lukić," he said. "Commissioner Milenković will be here any moment. He ordered that nothing be touched. We are taking over the case. Your investigation team has been told not to come. The commissioner asked for you to wait for him."

I nodded. "Where is the elevator?"

He pointed over his shoulder with his thumb. "On the ground floor. It's blocked. An elderly woman who lives on the fourth floor found the body. The elevator was on the fifth floor when she called it down from here. It was a shock when the doors opened, but she had enough presence of mind to call the police. We helped her climb up to her apartment."

"I'll just take a look," I said.

He unlocked the door to the building, opened it and moved aside. It was darker inside, making me pause to let my eyes adjust. I remembered awkwardly colliding with Miss Aksentijević there the night before. I had not forgotten where the switch was located. I pushed it and looked across the foyer.

At the other end, near the open elevator, stood a girl with unruly dark hair and a round face. She was wearing a short yellow t-shirt and tight black corduroy pants, low on her hips, baring a rather wide strip around her waist with her navel in the middle. Commissioner Milenković might have had too much understanding for the informal way his young colleagues dressed.

Without uttering a word or changing her expression, the girl just moved away, revealing the scene behind her.

At first it seemed there were several bodies on the elevator's red carpet. The three mirrors multiplied the face of the woman lying on her left side in a fetal position. She would not have fit in the small elevator stretched out. Her loose dark-green short-sleeved dress covered her completely like shroud. Her head was resting on her left biceps, the upright forearm leaning against the glass wall opposite the doors. Her hand was hanging like a large drooping flower. Red hair enveloped her face.

"Miss Ljubica Aksentijević, literary agent," said the girl, confirming what I already knew.

"Is she dead?" I said, not realizing until afterward how pointless it was to ask.

The girl eyed me guardedly before answering.

"There's no carotid pulse. We checked."

I crouched down by the entrance to the elevator and looked intently.

"Did you establish the cause of death? I don't see any external wound. At least not with the body in this position."

"We are not to move her."

"I know. If there is a wound, it certainly isn't big. Otherwise there would be blood."

"People die even without spilling blood."

Just as I was gazing inquisitively at the girl, there came the sound of the front door being unlocked and then opened. I turned around and saw Commissioner Milenković entering with a short, spare, middle-aged man with a receding hairline, wearing a dark-blue linen suit. He was carrying a large medical bag. I quickly got to my feet.

As they reached the elevator, the commissioner just glanced at me. The doctor crouched right down where I had been a moment before. He placed his bag on the floor, opened it, took out latex gloves and started putting them on. The commissioner exchanged a brief look with the girl and then signaled me with his head to follow him up the stairs. Not a word was spoken.

We continued in silence as we went up. I took advantage of the unexpected opportunity to count the steps for the first time during the day and in peace. I did not rely on my automatic counter but consciously counted them. If I had been alone, I would have done so in a low voice.

"Seventy-two stairs," gasped Commissioner Milenković, the first to break the silence as we got to the last floor, confirming the number I had also reached. "This is wearing me out."

We continued to Teodosijević's apartment. I glanced at the door to the neighboring apartment. The lock seemed properly sealed. The commissioner gave a short knock and the young man I had met the night before in the Communications Department appeared at the door almost at the same moment. He would have had to bow his head a little if he'd wanted to go out. He moved aside so we could enter, greeting me with a slight nod.

I followed the commissioner into the large room. He passed by the covered easel and sat on the edge of the cot where he had sat that morning. He rubbed his forehead with the tips of his fingers for several moments.

Then he sighed and motioned toward the brown arm-chair. I sat down there.

"I'm listening, Inspector Lukić," he said in a tired voice like a man who did not feel at all like talking.

"What do you want to know?"

"Who did you talk to after stopping on Chestnut Boulevard? And more importantly—what phone did you use?"

I reached into my left pants pocket and took out the gray cellphone.

"It rang on the back seat after I started driving. I assume they left it there earlier. Otherwise they would not have escaped your attention if they'd tried while my car was parked near Café Mocha."

Commissioner Milenković raised his eyes toward Stanislav Mirić who was standing at the entrance to the room. It suddenly occurred to me that the tall young man was the only associate who had ever introduced himself to me. He came and took the telephone from me, then headed for the window in the small room.

"Someone you knew?" asked the commissioner.

"No. A young woman's voice. I'd never heard it before."

"What did she want?"

"Jelena Jakovljević's new novel."

He stared at me briefly.

"The Grand Manuscript?"

I nodded.

There was another pause. "Are they behind the body in the elevator?"

"That's what they indicated."

"Why did Miss Aksentijević . . . die?"

"They wanted to establish whether she had read the novel. They put her to some test that, it seems, only the immortal can survive."

This time Commissioner Milenković rubbed his temples.

"Why is it that literature attracts so many lunatics?"

"There are quite a lot of them in the other arts too, but they stay below the National Security Agency's radar."

"I'd be happy to let you handle this too if it wasn't for that damn telephone without a SIM card and battery. And not just the phone. . . ." He turned toward the small room. "What do we have this time?"

Mirić went up to him holding the cellphone in his outstretched hand.

"A cheap model. No modifications."

The commissioner motioned his head toward me. The young man came up again and handed me the telephone, then went out into the small hall.

"I thought you would hold onto it," I said.

"Why take away your only contact with them? It's in everyone's interest to maintain it. And even if we took it away from you, before long you'd find a new one in your car or some other place." He paused. "We're dealing with serious lunatics here. They should not be underestimated."

"I would have expected them to use better equipment. If it's possible to tap police cellphones, what's to be said about such toys?"

"They don't care if we tap them. They feel they have the upper hand. They killed Miss Aksentijević right under my nose. Or they brought her body here without being seen. It was in the elevator on the fifth floor and none of my people noticed it."

As I put the telephone back in my left pants pocket, my right pocket vibrated. In my confusion I almost reached for it.

"Why did they call you?" asked the commissioner.

"They're continuing their search for the manuscript after it turned out that Miss Aksentijević didn't have it. Now they think it's with me."

"Is it?" he asked in a softer voice.

"No."

I held out under his long inquisitive look.

"We must have true cooperation, Inspector Lukić. Otherwise I will not be able to protect you. And you need my protection. These lunatics are not only serious, they're dangerous too, as we have just seen. They will not be deterred at all by the fact that you are a policeman."

I felt like putting Commissioner Milenković's mind at ease. A ruthless publisher, not dangerous lunatics, was behind it all. I did not mention this hypothesis, however, because the cracks in it were getting too big. It was no longer about just three unanswered questions. Miss Aksentijević's murder certainly did not fit into the idea of an ad campaign. Publishers were indeed ruthless, but there's a limit to everything. Something quite different was going on, something that could definitely be dangerous.

"Of course we will cooperate," I replied with a nod, then got up and headed for the front door that Mirić had already opened for me. I was stopped by the commissioner's voice. What he said was the last thing I expected to hear from him.

"Take care of yourself." The tone was gentle, paternal.

Puzzled, I just smiled and went out. In the corridor my conscience bothered me for not saying anything in return.

As soon as I was in the stairwell, I took the cellphone out of my right pants pocket. Again there was no written message. The same picture as last time was on the screen: the yellow ducky on the bottom of the bathtub. But there was no time to go deeper into this riddle because my inside jacket pocket started ringing. I only realized it was my private cell when I took it out. No call number was given.

"Hello?"

"Hello, Inspector Lukić," said a voice that I had been firmly convinced I would never hear again.

"HELLO," I REPLIED IN confusion, although that was surely not the correct response to the man who had almost killed me. There was no doubt in my mind. His deep voice was as distinctive as fingerprints.

We had met twice before but I still didn't know what he looked like. Both times his face had been concealed by the hood of his white robe—the regalia of the Last Book secret society's Grand Master. Our paths had crossed first in the underground amphitheater of a villa and then in the corridor that connected two realities. Commissioner Milenković's sudden arrival had saved me at the last moment in the amphitheater, while I had been in no danger in the corridor. Although seen just briefly, the tableau of fifteen motionless figures in brown robes sitting at a long table with one in white at the head was etched in my memory forever.

I had heard nothing about the secret society since the end of the "Last Book" case. The investigators had not seemed very interested in it even though I'd described in detail what I'd gone through in the amphitheater and corridor, and the members I had met. Vera told me that none of them had dropped by the Papyrus during the short time the bookstore was still open.

"I hope you remember me," said the Grand Master.

"How could I forget the man who tried to kill me?"

He laughed resoundingly. "Kill you? How did I try to kill you?"

"You know perfectly well. You lowered *The Last Book* open toward my face."

"Yes, I lowered an open book, but why do you think it was *The Last Book*?"

"You said it was." I stopped, realizing this was not enough, and added, "It had a blue cover."

"Lots of books have a blue cover."

"It had to be *The Last Book*. You would've been in a tight spot if it had been any other book. If you'd managed to bring it close to my face, what would you have said to the secret society members when the book didn't have the effect everyone expected, announced by none other than you?"

"There was no danger of my bringing it close to your face. I knew that the arrival of National Security agents would get me out of that tight spot."

"You could not have known that they would turn up, let alone when."

"Do you think so? You underestimate me, Inspector Lukić."

"And you underestimate me if you expect me to believe the unbelievable."

"But you did believe that an unbelievable coincidence took place—the agents arrived just as I was lowering the book toward you. Rescuers appear at the last moment like that only in second-rate detective stories."

"And *The Last Book*, of course, is not that."

"Of course it isn't, although the main character turned out to be rather credulous."

"Did you call me to tell me that?"

"No, something else. I did not try to kill you; on the contrary, your safety has always been uppermost in my mind. You are extremely important for our society. If it were religious we would have already proclaimed you a saint. Without you *The Last Book* would not exist."

"That's not exactly how it looked to me down in that amphitheater."

"Nothing was as it seemed there. But let's not talk about the past. Your safety is in much greater jeopardy now than it appeared to you to be in the villa."

"You don't say."

"Are you really so credulous? Even after Miss Aksentijević's murder?"

I thought of asking him how he knew about the

murder, but I was sure he wouldn't tell me. Then I would have looked naive indeed.

That's when I reached the ground floor. No one was there. I looked across the foyer. The long-haired young man was no longer standing in front of the door. The display above the elevator indicated that it was still down there. I stopped beside the closed door. It would be better to remain inside the building until I had finished the conversation.

"Perhaps you would enlighten a credulous inspector. Why would his safety be jeopardized after Miss Aksentijević's murder?"

"Your sarcasm is out of place. You know the answer perfectly well. You have something that many people are looking for. They will stop at nothing to get hold of it."

"And that is . . . ?"

"What's the purpose of this game, Inspector Lukić? We don't have time for it. You are in serious danger. You have the Grand Manuscript, of course."

"No, I don't."

A few moments passed in silence before a loud sigh came from the phone.

"All right, you don't, if that's the way you want it. But it actually makes no difference. What's important is that they are convinced you do. Miss Aksentijević didn't have it either, but she paid for it with her life anyway."

"They?"

"The people who believe in the Grand Manuscript."

"Just like you believe in the Last Book?"

"More or less."

"So that's another secret society devoted to a book? You've got competition."

"It's not a good idea to take secret societies lightly. I thought you already realized that. Our belief has turned out to be true."

"Maybe it escaped my attention, but I don't see any end of the world."

"It escaped your attention because the end can come in various forms. The world is certainly not the same since the advent of the Last Book."

"You should do your competition a favor and tell them about it. They are confident that the first person to read the Grand Manuscript will become immortal. And what's the good of being immortal if the end of the world is nigh?"

There was a moment of silence. When the Grand Master spoke again, his voice was hushed.

"Immortality is the only way to survive the end of the world."

"So that's it. Then the Grand Manuscript has even greater value. It's no wonder so many people are interested in it. How about you? Are you interested in it too?"

There was another brief silence.

"We are only interested in protecting you."

"I've never heard of a saint being offered protection. Usually it's the other way around. Saints are the protectors."

"I won't hold this mockery against you. Not all saints are wise. They include the naive who don't realize what danger looms ahead and so they make fun of it instead of eagerly accepting the protection they are offered."

"What kind of protection are you offering me?"

"It's certainly better than what the police would provide. Even the secret police. We would take you somewhere safe. Beyond the reach of people looking for the Grand Manuscript. Only a secret society can save you from another secret society."

I sighed.

"You really do think I'm naive if you expect me to swallow that story. What you're interested in, of course, is not my safety but the Grand Manuscript. You're convinced I have it and you want to get your hands on it before the others do. But you're wasting your time. As I told you, I've never set eyes on it. It makes no difference whether you believe me or not. Thank you for your offer of protection."

He sighed in return.

"I'm sorry it turned out like this. It would be much easier if we cooperated. But there's nothing to be done. We'll have to protect you even against your will. Regardless of what you think about our motives, your protection is a priority for us." He paused and then added on a lighter note, "I look forward to seeing you again soon, Inspector Lukić."

The line went dead before I could say anything. How strange, I thought. The secret police and a secret society have offered me protection at the same time, and both are dissatisfied with my cooperation.

I put the phone back in my jacket pocket and headed for the exit. On emerging I squinted at the bright sunlight. I unlocked the car door but did not get inside. I checked the back seat and then looked all around me. I didn't notice anything suspicious, least of all Commissioner Milenković's people. I knew, however, that they were somewhere nearby, keeping a close eye on me. For the first time, I was pleased about it.

I got in behind the wheel. Just as I turned on the engine, my jacket pocket rang again. How much simpler my life had been when I had had just one cell with me. With four, I would spend most of the day on the phone.

∽ 28 ∾

"Chief Inspector Đorđević" was written on the screen of my service cellphone.

"Hello."

"Hello, Inspector Lukić. Can you talk?"

"Yes, go ahead."

"What's this murder we've got?"

"Miss Ljubica Aksentijević was murdered, a literary agent."

"Agent? What do literary agents do? Forgive my lack of knowledge."

"No problem. They represent writers as a go-between with publishers."

"Oh, I see. Is a literary agent's work also so dangerous that they could lose their life?"

"Not usually. This is actually the first such case to my knowledge."

"The case file says she called us last night and you went to do an on-site investigation. What was it about?"

"She suspected that something had happened to the writer she represents . . . Miss Jelena Jakovljević. She couldn't enter her apartment because it was locked from the inside. But the apartment turned out to be empty."

"How's that possible?"

"Not even Inspector Vesić could explain it. He opened the door for me."

"So where's the writer?"

"She's disappeared."

"Interesting. And then there was a break-in at the same apartment, right?"

"That's right. They searched it thoroughly."

"Very thoroughly indeed. I saw the photographs. What were the burglars looking for?"

"By general consensus, the manuscript of Miss Jakovljević's new novel."

"Is it that important?"

"Big money is at stake."

"I never imagined there was big money in literature."

"Usually there isn't. Detective novels are the only exception. Our profession."

"You don't say. Nice. Does Miss Aksentijević's murder have anything to do with the manuscript?"

"It seems so. Someone is very anxious to get hold of it."

"Do you have any indication as to who it might be?"

"No one specific, although they made contact with me. Anonymously. Miss Aksentijević didn't have what they were looking for, so they can be expected to continue their search."

"Another murder?" asked the chief inspector after a slight hesitation.

"It shouldn't be ruled out."

"We've got to do everything we can to prevent that. You'll get reinforcements right away."

"That might not be necessary. The National Security Agency has taken over the forensic examination of Miss Aksentijević's body and just might take over the entire case."

"Oh, yes. I almost forgot about them. They joined in last night, right? What caught their attention? The case is unusual, but it's certainly not the type that interests the Agency. At least apparently."

Now I was the one to hesitate.

"I have no idea what caught their attention. They didn't say. As you know, they're not inclined to explain."

"Yes, they're not inclined at all. Although it would be easier for everyone if we cooperated. Well, we can't do a thing about it. In any case, if you need any help, let me know right away. And keep me informed of any new developments."

"By all means."

I waited for him to hang up first, but he had something more to say.

"Take care of yourself, Inspector Lukić. The Agency has a reason for getting involved, and literature isn't harmless, as you know."

"Everything will be fine," I replied, trying to sound self-confident.

Before returning the cell to my jacket pocket, I looked at the clock in the upper right-hand corner of the screen. Twenty-five to three. It was later than I had thought.

As I drove to police headquarters, I glanced at the rear-view mirror repeatedly. Traffic had lightened up a bit so it was easier to check behind. No one seemed to be following me, but I knew that was a false impression. Commissioner Milenković's people were certainly around. If anyone else was there, they would have to be really adept to dodge both my attention and theirs.

After getting out of the car, I looked around the garage, flooded by bright neon lights. It would not have crossed my mind before, but now it was obvious: I was alone. There were only a few parked cars in the large space with its rows of square pillars. My steps echoed hollowly as I made my way toward the elevator.

I had the impression that someone was stealthily watching me—and not just the cameras that covered the whole garage. In the past I had ridiculed such B movie clichés, but that didn't ease the anxiety that filled me now. It was not until the elevator was taking me to the fifth floor that I breathed more easily.

After sitting down at my desk, I turned on the computer and called Inspector Prokopović. I told him I was back and did not expect to go out again, and would soon be coming to the duty room. He briefly informed me that there were still no emergencies. If it weren't for the case I was working on, it would have been a very calm Saturday.

I opened the message that Inspector Kostić had sent that morning and a chessboard of little pictures filled the screen. I clicked on the last one and its enlargement replaced the grid of thumbnails. Bringing my head a little closer, I stared at the ducky on the bottom of the bathtub. I stayed that way around half a minute and then my right pants pocket started vibrating.

I hesitated just a moment and then took out the cellphone and pressed the button that opened messages.

"Well?" was what the new one said.

"Well, what?" I replied.

"Haven't you seen it yet?"

"What?"

"Does famous Inspector Dejan Lukić need help seeing the obvious?"

"Did I ask for help? Why on earth did you send me a photograph of the ducky? And not only once but twice?"

"Because the novel can't wait for you to figure it out for yourself. Someone might come to harm because of your poor insight. Even twice was not enough for you."

"If you care so much about the novel, doesn't its narrative coherence suffer when the writer openly helps the main character?"

"It suffers, but there's nothing to be done. Of two evils, I accepted the one that seemed lesser to me. If at least I had been of some help . . ."

"A good writer would not be in the awkward position of choosing between two evils. . . ."

"That was low."

"That bit about my poor insight was not very high either."

For the first time since we started exchanging messages, I did not receive a reply almost immediately. A good fifteen seconds passed before it came.

"You're right, Inspector Dejan Lukić. The novel has to be my top priority. I must not subordinate it to a main character. So the best thing is to stop helping you. From now on you'll have to manage on your own as best you can."

"That's what I've been doing. You just said that you haven't really helped me."

"Please don't cry for help when you get in trouble. And you will for sure."

"Rest assured there will be no cries for help. I'm in the habit of getting myself out of trouble."

I expected another message, but the seconds passed and nothing appeared on the screen. My eyes remained fixed on the clock in the corner. Two minutes later I put the phone in my pocket and sighed.

Perhaps this should have been avoided, but now it was too late. That's the usual outcome when two egos collide. Very well, let's see how an inspector with poor insight manages on his own. I returned my gaze to the ducky on the large screen.

Ten minutes later I reached for the mouse to close the photograph's window. It made no sense to keep on staring. I would not see anything because there was nothing to see. I had naively let my mysterious SMS collocutor trifle with my pride. She must be gloating now.

The cursor was already on the x-spot when my hand suddenly stopped. I looked at the same picture on the screen, but as though with different eyes. All at once I clearly saw what had persistently eluded me before. It was indeed obvious, just as she had said. So obvious that instead of being thrilled, I felt a twinge of frustration.

∽ 29 ∾

THE DUCKY WAS STILL where I'd seen it the first time, but was not looking in the same direction. Like a little arrow, its beak now pointed right, not left. The difference became evident just a moment before I closed the window, when the picture on the screen overlapped with the one that finally surfaced from my memory. I might not have the fastest recollection, but it was reliable and had never let me down. Someone had turned the yellow rubber toy around.

Who could have done it? And no less important, why? After my two visits, there had been the burglar—or several of them—and then inspectors Zarić and Kostić. The cleaning lady had found the door ajar, which would have made entry easy after the burglar's departure. But I didn't think anyone else had entered, and it was unlikely that Mrs. Sokolović had lied when she said she'd just peeked inside.

The burglar was primarily interested in books and there weren't any in the bathroom. If they went in there at all, they didn't move the curtain. The first picture that Inspector Kostić took in the bathroom showed it was pulled over the bathtub. Whoever had made such a mess in the rest of the apartment certainly would not have been careful to pull the curtain closed after pulling it aside, let alone waste time turning the ducky around.

I could have called my two colleagues and asked whether anyone had touched the rubber ducky—or just Kostić, who had taken the picture, since Zarić had only been inside the apartment for a brief time. But I didn't have to; both were experienced inspectors who would never slip up and move something on the site of an investigation. Let alone photograph it afterward.

None of those who could have turned the ducky around had any reason to do so, and yet there it was, turned around. This was a new riddle. Had I noted it by myself, I might have put it aside temporarily. It would seem less important than the larger riddles whose resolution had precedence. But the mysterious person I had exchanged SMS messages with over an impossible cellphone didn't think so. The riddle of the rubber toy was clearly very important to them since they had broken off contact with me because of it, rightfully accusing me of poor insight.

Was it nonetheless possible that someone had entered the apartment after the burglar had left? There certainly were candidates. Many parties were interested in Jelena Jakovljević's ninth manuscript. Their job would have been easier because they wouldn't have had to break into an unlocked apartment, and their traces would be invisible in the chaos left behind by the previous visitor. But even if that were so, there was no answer to the key question: why would anyone touch the yellow ducky?

My eyes were still trained on the large photograph on the screen. Something else started wriggling in the depths of my memory. I made a concerted effort, but what emerged was something I already knew: the picture I was looking at and the one I remembered overlapped each other, creating a two-headed ducky.

Something, however, was different, but it took some time before I realized what it was. The first time they overlapped, the head on the photograph was sharper than the other one, as recollections tend to be hazier. Now the heads were equally hazy as though both had come from my memory.

And that's when it hit me. Both overlapping pictures had truly come from my memory. I had seen the ducky with its head turned left when I first entered the apartment of the person masquerading as Jelena Jakovljević. The first time I saw it turned right was not on Kostić's photograph but during my second visit, when I entered the bathroom briefly. I would never have noted this by myself had I not been put on the right trail.

So someone had turned the ducky around much earlier, between my two visits, not during the night after the burglar had left. That meant that the alleged Mr. Teodosijević had not been lying when he told me there was someone in the apartment next door. It had not been just an excuse to lure me back.

Who could it be? Who had unlocked the door and entered the apartment so silently that even Adam had almost missed it? Who had frightened the fake painter so much that he'd had no other choice than to call the police, even though their presence was not the least in his favor? And above all, who had turned the yellow toy around in the bathtub in order to leave a trace of their visit for those skilled enough to detect it?

I felt my hackles rise when the realization struck me.

It was not smug excitement that filled me, however, but disquiet at the terrible possibility that it had come too late. Part of the message from my anonymous SMS collocutor flashed before my eyes:

"Someone might come to harm because of your poor insight."

⌒ 30 ⌒

I REACHED FEVERISHLY INTO my jacket pocket and took out my service cellphone. My thumb danced about the keypad searching for Inspector Vesić's phone number. It soon appeared on the screen, but I didn't push the call button. A sudden thought stayed my finger at the last moment.

I had to assume that whoever killed the literary agent was able to tap police communications. Regardless of how they did it. Let Commissioner Milenković tackle the problem. I didn't dare say anything to Inspector Vesić that would make him look suspicious in their eyes.

Judging by our only conversation, they didn't realize that Vesić had been in Jelena Jakovljević's apartment between my two visits. If they had, they would have tried to get hold of him before Miss Aksentijević. They had put her to a lethal test because she might have had something to do with last night's break-in. But he had entered the apartment much earlier, so the prospects were greater that he was the one who had gotten hold of the *Find Me* file.

They did know, however, that three visits had taken place before the break-in and that I was not there all three times. The young woman who had called while I was driving down Chestnut Boulevard mentioned the two times I went in. The only witness to Vesić's visit was the alleged painter Teodosijević and he—it was now certain—was a member of the Grand Manuscript secret society.

Blind or not, he could not have seen Vesić because the inspector did not turn on the lights when he went back into the building after the two of us parted. He got along equally well in the dark and had wanted to stay hidden. So the secret society was searching for the mysterious second visitor. They might subject them to the test even before me owing to the mystery cloaking them.

If the phony painter wasn't blind, however, then he'd seen Vesić the first time he was in the building with Miss Aksentijević and me. He had probably been watching us the whole time through the peephole and seen the inspector's skill for himself: using just two little picks, he had quickly handled the front door that was locked from the inside. Sooner or later he was certain to connect Vesić to the second visit. It was actually strange that it had not yet happened.

I pushed the call button. My conversation with Inspector Vesić had to be as innocuous as possible so that the inquisitive ears most likely listening would not suspect anything. The phone started ringing. When no one answered after the fourth ring, I felt tightness in my chest. The call was finally answered after the sixth ring, and I let out a sigh of relief.

"Hello, Inspector Lukić," said Vesić.

"Hello, how are you?"

"Very well, and you?"

"My shift is almost over and then I'll be very well too."

"An exhausting Saturday?"

"Unusual. Nevertheless, I managed to get hold of what you asked for."

A short pause followed.

"You did?"

"For your collection."

"Ah, my collection."

"The yellow rubber ducky that you're missing."

Again there was a lapse before he spoke.

"Was it hard to find?"

"It wasn't easy, but anything for an esteemed colleague. Shall we meet for a moment so I can give it to you? Then you won't have to wait until Monday."

"Sure. I have to go downtown anyway. Where would you like to meet? And when?"

I looked at the clock at the bottom of the monitor.

"Now it's seventeen minutes to four. How about if we meet at four-fifteen at the same place we parted last night?"

"In front of the entrance?"

"Yes."

"I think I can make it."

"Wonderful. See you there."

"See you soon, Inspector Lukić. And thanks for the ducky."

"You're welcome."

I expected Commissioner Milenković to call me as soon as I put my service cell back in my pocket, but none of my telephones rang. He had certainly been listening to our conversation and easily caught on to the fact that it should not be taken literally. He also knew that the photograph of the ducky in the bathtub had been on my monitor for some time. It would not be hard for him to make the connection and realize that Inspector Vesić had been in apartment 19 last night too.

On second thought, the commissioner had no reason to call me. All he could do was rebuke me for not calling him first to report what I had discovered about Vesić, but he would just be wasting his time. Taking care of Vesić's safety was his most urgent issue now. If members of the Grand Manuscript secret society had also tapped my service cell, they might have come to their own conclusions about the identity of the mysterious second visitor. In that case, Inspector Vesić would indeed be in great danger.

I nevertheless trusted this was not the case. Without the photograph of the ducky, they didn't have the key to our coded conversation. They might have found it unusual, but it would stay covert. And they had no access to the photograph in the closed police communications system. I had to believe that, otherwise we would be in a quandary that greatly surpassed this case.

Perhaps I really should have called the commissioner first, but I had been seized by the fear that something had already happened to Inspector Vesić. I'd been under the influence of the insinuation in my unknown collocutor's SMS. In my excitement, it had not occurred to me that another untapped phone could be used to check whether the inspector was all right.

Well, that could not be changed. I would soon be seeing Vesić, and the commissioner would be there as well with his people, so we would get the inspector to safety right away. Members of the Grand Manuscript society would probably be in the vicinity too. They would have had no trouble figuring out where we were meeting, even though no place was mentioned. But their hands would be tied with the National Security Agency there. This was all I had left to hope for.

Before turning off the computer, I glanced at the clock in the lower right-hand corner of the monitor again. Nine minutes to four. I needed about ten minutes to get to Oak Street. I would go there at once, finding it easier to wait in front of the building than here. I called Inspector Prokopović again and told him that I would not be seeing him today after all, and then headed for the elevators.

My jacket started ringing just as I entered the empty garage.

As I RUSHED TOWARD my car, I took out my private cellphone with a frown. With four telephones in my pockets and the way things were going, it was a real wonder that no one had called me since Chief Inspector Đorđević more than an hour ago. But whoever was calling this phone had chosen the wrong moment. I was not at all in the mood for a private conversation.

I didn't recognize the number that appeared on the screen. I was just about to push the answer button when a thought cut me short: perhaps they were trying to distract me. They were calling me while I was in the garage to put me off my guard. If a trap had been set for me there, I would fall into it more readily if I was preoccupied with telephoning.

I stopped and looked around me as the sharp ring continued to reverberate in the large echoing space. Just like the last time, it seemed no one was there. I tried to remember the parked cars I'd seen. I would have said there weren't any new ones, but I might have been wrong.

I continued cautiously toward my car and finally answered.

"Hello?"

"Inspector Dejan Lukić?" asked a female voice. The only people who spoke so cordially were telemarketers trying to sell me something I had no desire to buy.

"Yes," I replied in a voice that was the exact opposite of hers.

"Nice to meet you!" continued the woman, who sounded of indefinite age. My icy tone had done nothing to decrease her friendliness. "My name is Leposava Žutić. I'm from Magnifying Glass Press."

She paused as though waiting to see what impression her words had made.

"That's nice, Miss or Mrs. Žutić, but right now I

don't have time to talk about publishing. I'm in a terrible rush."

"Of course, Inspector. I understand you completely. So I'll be quite brief. I'm calling about the manuscript of the novel *Find Me*. Magnifying Glass is very interested. . . ."

"I will be even briefer," I said, interrupting her. "I don't have the manuscript."

"You haven't heard our proposal. . . ."

"And I won't hear it either."

I turned off the phone with a sharp jab and put it back in my jacket pocket, then reached for the car keys. I felt bad about cutting her off so rudely, but I'd had no choice. Regardless of whether the conversation was polite or impolite, it would have ended the same way. There was no reason for it to go on for ten minutes.

Before getting into the car, I checked the back seat. This had already become a conditioned reflex. As I unlocked the door, my private cell started ringing again. I took it out, ascertained that it was the same number as before, then turned off the call. If she persisted, I would have to caution her. I would be reluctant to resort to this, but with some people you had to take off the kid gloves. Luckily, she seemed to realize it was pointless to insist.

Once behind the wheel, I hesitated a moment about using the rotating light, then decided not to. It would make me unnecessarily conspicuous and I would not get there much faster. It was lunchtime, so rush-hour was probably over.

The thought of lunch reminded me of what I'd been pushing to the back of my mind for some time. I had barely put anything into my mouth that morning and had skipped dinner the night before. This case really had no consideration for hunger. My stomach had growled two or three times since I'd gone back to the office. Even though there'd been almost no letup, I would have found at least the time to pick up a sand-wich in the second-floor restaurant. Unfortunately, it didn't open on Saturday. Under other circumstances, I would have asked Inspector Vesić to have lunch with me, but Commissioner Milenković would be unlikely to go along with it. Forget it, I thought, I'll have to eat alone, as usual.

I concentrated on getting there as soon as possible and didn't pay much attention to whether anyone was following me. It wasn't even necessary. Traffic had in-deed lightened and someone tailing me for any length of time would easily have caught my eye. In any case, even if I had noted someone, I wouldn't have done any-thing. They all knew where I was headed, so it made no difference if I was being followed.

I reached Oak Street at 16:07. This time I found two free parking places. I parked in one, got out of the car and headed for the entrance. The front of the building was still in sunlight, but it was not as bright as before. I stood beside the door and scanned the surroundings. Several passers-by were going their own way. The calls of children came from somewhere. Nothing seemed out of the ordinary, but I hadn't expected it to be.

I thought of calling Vesić to see how far he'd gotten, but it would not have been wise. He would get there all the more safely the less we were in contact. Further-more, Commissioner Milenković was surely keeping an eye on him. I would have to be patient a little longer.

I hated admitting it, but my mysterious SMS col-locutor was right. I should have been more insightful. Even without their help I should have deduced that Inspector Vesić had gone into apartment 19 last night after my first time there. He'd had an excellent motive for doing so.

He had not been enticed there by the same thing that interested the others, ranging from the secret society to this Magnifying Glass Press that was clearly ready to loosen its purse strings to get the better of the competition. He had known nothing about the novel *Find Me*. Neither Miss Aksentijević nor I had mentioned Jelena Jakovljević's new book in front of him, and when the two of us were together not even I had known anything about the Grand Manuscript.

He'd taken advantage of the fact that his car was parked slightly farther away, had headed toward it but had not left. He had waited for me to drive off and then gone back inside the building. He'd had little trouble entering the apartment without being seen. What compelled him was the urge to decipher something far more important to him than any manuscript, the greatest enigma for those who "have a special interest in locks," as he had nicely put it: how could an apartment that was locked from the inside be empty?

Had he discovered something there? If he had, he would not have called to tell me because he would have wanted to hide the fact that he'd been in the apartment. Well, almost. He'd left the trademark of his visit—the turned around ducky. He would tell me whether he had solved the mystery if I discovered his trademark. He had always been inclined to such games. Well, I had discovered his trademark. Not exactly on my own, but that was of no consequence. Soon I would find out whether the empty apartment locked from the inside was the result of a hoax or magic. And also whether Inspector Vesić had possibly found something else that had escaped my attention.

I looked at my wristwatch—16:19. He should be there any minute. Last night it had taken him about forty minutes. It suddenly occurred to me that I'd taken it for granted he was leaving from home, which wasn't necessarily the case. The problem with cellphones was that you never knew the other person's whereabouts. Indeed, he'd said he thought he could make it by 16:15, so it was probable that I'd found him at home after all. I stayed there waiting by the entrance, periodically shifting my weight from one foot to the other. Everything around me still seemed ordinary.

At 16:26 I finally lost patience, hounded by a sense of foreboding. I would call Commissioner Milenković. If he rebuked me for calling him, I would reply that I'd imagined cooperation meant his not keeping me on tenterhooks in this way. If he wanted to avoid any telephoning, there were other ways to let me know discreetly what had happened to Inspector Vesić, and not leave me to wait indefinitely. Several of his people had to be in the vicinity.

Just as my hand started for my jacket pocket to take out my service cell, the telephone in my left pants pocket went off. It didn't sound like it had on the back seat of the car, however. What came out was like a muted gong. I quickly lowered my raised hand toward my pants.

It took a few moments to figure out what to press to open the SMS message. There was no text and I had to bring the gray phone a little closer to get a better view of the photograph. Even so, I couldn't tell what it was right away. At first it appeared to be an abstract picture full of straight lines and symmetry. It took a good fifteen seconds before I finally realized what I was looking at.

On the floor of the elevator in the building behind my back lay Inspector Vesić's briefcase in triple reflection. Open and empty.

∼ 32 ∽

I PUT THE GRAY telephone promptly back into my left pants pocket and started feverishly searching through the others for the key to the building's front door. This would ordinarily not be necessary because I prided myself on my keen memory. With just a fraction more self-possession I would have immediately remembered which pocket it was in, but I seemed to have suddenly lost my presence of mind.

When I finally found the key, I couldn't get it into the keyhole because my fingers refused to obey. This hadn't happened to me in a long time. Luckily there was no one nearby to see a police inspector barely keeping his trembling under control. When I finally got into the foyer, I didn't waste even the moment it would have taken to turn on the lights in passing, even though I knew it would take a little time for my pupils to adjust to the weak light inside. Heedless of the noise I made, I ran the short distance to the elevator.

First I banged unnecessarily hard on the call button, and only then raised my eyes to the display. The elevator had just started down from the fifth floor. Although it traveled at its normal speed, it now seemed unbearably slow to me.

I had never thought I would ever see Inspector Vesić's briefcase open. Had circumstances been otherwise, my chief interest would have been to know what was in it. It was known to contain something heavy, but no one had any idea what could be so important for him to carry it with him at all times. Certainly not burglary tools, because two little picks were all he needed to take care of any lock.

Right then, however, what interested me was not the contents of the mysterious briefcase, but the fate of Inspector Vesić himself. The picture of the empty briefcase sent to the gray telephone clearly indicated who had hold of him. How was that possible? How had they outwitted the National Security Agency? Commissioner Milenković knew he was facing a serious and dangerous opponent, but still it shouldn't have happened. No secret society should be a match for the secret police.

There was yet another puzzle. Even if they had managed to outsmart the Agency, how had they reached the building and unlocked the three security locks so as to take the picture of the empty briefcase in the elevator? I had spent most of the past half-hour in front of the building. In all that time only one elderly couple had emerged. True, they could have entered by the back door, but presumably it was under surveillance.

A thought suddenly crossed my mind that made possible all that was seemingly impossible. The secret society could easily have gotten hold of Vesić, reached the building in time and effortlessly unlocked the three locks that had given many people a headache—provided that nothing had to be done by force. If they could count on Vesić's cooperation.

There was no chance to give this crazy idea more attention, however, because the elevator had almost reached the ground floor and squealing tires could be heard behind me. Swiftly, I turned my head, in time to see a light-red car stop in front of the entrance. Car doors started opening even before it had reached a standstill and four young people quickly got out. If I hadn't recognized them, I might have thought they were rushing to an afternoon party in the building.

Unlocking the front door, the first to enter the foyer was the long-haired young man in a brick-colored sweatshirt, followed by the girl photographer and the couple I had first seen in Café Mocha.

"Don't touch anything, Inspector Lukić," said the lad in loosely laced trainers at the forefront, almost shouting.

I was about to reply that I had no reason to touch an empty briefcase, when I looked round again—and was at a loss for words. The elevator had meanwhile reached the ground floor. The noise from the entrance had drowned out the already soft sound of the doors opening. Lying on the floor of the elevator was not the briefcase but its owner.

He was curled up, like Miss Aksentijević. Nor was his face visible—a hat covered it instead of hair—but there was no doubt as to who it was. The elegant black suit and large dark-red bow tie that had distinguished his appearance now seemed somewhat grotesque on the elevator's dark carpeting.

Uncertain what question to ask first, my eyes slid in confusion over the commissioner's four young associates who had gathered around the entrance to the elevator.

"Let us take care of this, Inspector Lukić," said the photographer. "Commissioner Milenković is waiting for you in the car." She nodded toward the foyer.

Instead of leaving, I looked at the elevator again. Something deep inside me fought against leaving just like that, turning my back on my dead colleague. My conscience stung me with an almost physical pain. How could I have thought for a moment that Inspector Vesić was in collusion with the secret society?

I felt a hand touch my shoulder lightly. This time the photographer did not say anything, but her smile expressed more than condolence. Slowly I made my way to the exit.

∽ 33 ∾

THE FORENSIC DOCTOR IN a dark-blue linen suit, whom I'd met there a little over two hours ago, appeared at the entrance just as I was leaving. He thanked me with a brief nod for opening the door and holding it for him, and then hurried past me toward the elevator.

I squinted again when I got outside. Shading my eyes with my hand, I stooped slightly to look inside the light-red car. It didn't surprise me that the Agency had started using such flashy cars. Everything was upside-down with them. They had been most conspicuous when trying to be least so. Instead of the somber colors that used to catch everyone's eye, these bright hues matched the Agency's fresh blood and did not stand out at all.

Commissioner Milenković was sitting on the right-hand side of the back seat. I opened the left-hand door and got in next to him. We regarded each other for several moments without speaking.

"It is extremely important that you tell me everything you've left out, Inspector Lukić," said the commissioner, breaking the silence. "I mean everything." He spoke in an even tone as though we were making small-talk.

I pointed at the building's entrance. "A police inspector is lying in there dead, Commissioner Milenković." Even though I tried to speak calmly too, my voice trembled. "How about if you tell me why you let it happen?"

"I could ask you the same thing."

"How could I have prevented Vesić's murder?"

"You should not have telephoned him. You've been going it alone since the beginning instead of cooperating with me. We might have been able to save him if you'd contacted me as soon as you found out he'd been in that apartment upstairs last night." He paused. "Although I doubt we would have succeeded."

"You doubt that the National Security Agency is capable of handling a secret society?"

"The Agency is powerful but not almighty. The secret society probably suspected that Vesić was in the apartment between your two visits. Your unnecessary call only confirmed that. They had a big advantage. Obviously they'd been keeping an eye on him for some time and had no trouble getting hold of him before us. We found out where he was through his cell, but didn't get there in time. By the way, he was here in the vicinity."

"In the vicinity? Then why did he tell me he thought he could get here in half an hour?"

"Who knows? Maybe he realized they were closing in on him and tried to confuse them."

"Let's say it was like that. Then how did they bring

him . . . or carry him . . . into the building? As you know, I've been here since seven minutes past four, and I'm sure you still have both entrances under surveillance. Did you see anything?"

"No, we didn't, but that's of lesser importance. There must be another entrance, a secret one perhaps."

"What do you intend to do now? Are you going to catch these lunatics or will you hand the case over to us? They've already committed two murders and it's quite possible they won't stop there."

Just then two young men in jeans and orange teeshirts moved toward the entrance. They looked like repairmen who had come to fix something in the building. One was carrying a large black plastic box resembling a toolbox and the other was holding something upright that looked like two poles wrapped in olive-green cloth. Only an expert eye could recognize a folded stretcher. They knocked on the door and the girl with a mole on the tip of her nose soon opened it.

"We'll take care of the lunatics, Inspector Lukić," said Commissioner Milenković after the young men had gone inside. "But a much bigger problem has cropped up. Everything else is now secondary. Even the murder of a police inspector."

"What problem?" I asked, bewildered.

"The telephone has disappeared."

"Which telephone?"

The commissioner sighed like a teacher questioning a dim-witted schoolboy.

"The telephone that works without a SIM card and battery. The one you claim you found upstairs in the apartment. The damn telephone that got me into all this."

"What do you mean—disappeared?"

"Disappeared. Vanished into thin air. From a place where nothing can disappear. There is no safer repository in this country than the National Security Agency's safe."

I looked at him in disbelief.

"That's impossible. Nothing can disappear from your safe."

"No, it can't."

"So how . . . ?"

The commissioner shrugged his shoulders.

"I don't know. I'm hoping that you'll be able to tell me."

"Me? How in the world would I know?"

"I've run out of both the time and patience to play hide-and-seek with you, Inspector. I want a plain answer to the question I'm about to ask you. Is this another case like that?"

"Like what?"

"Like the 'Last Book.' Crossing realities. I see no other explanation for the appearance or disappearance of that impossible telephone unless someone from another reality is behind it. Another wizard-like writer playing irresponsibly with our reality."

We sat there in silence for about ten seconds.

"I don't think Occam would have liked that explanation," I said at last.

"Leave Occam out of it. It was a lot easier for him than it is for me. He had a much simpler world in mind. Well?"

"Why do you think I have the answer to that question?"

"Because everything revolved around you the first time too. Because as soon as I saw you in the Communications Department last night, my intuition told me that something exceptional was in the works. Because I have an unmistakable hunch that you've been hiding something from me from the beginning. What haven't you told me, Inspector Lukić? We've played at cooperation long enough. This is the last chance to take it seriously."

The door to the building opened and the forensic

doctor came out followed by the two girls. Then came the young men in orange teeshirts carrying a large black bulging plastic bag with closed zippers on the unfolded stretcher. The lads with short and long hair were the last to come out.

They all headed to the parking area. I felt a lump in my throat and rose up on the seat, leaning on my right hand so I could see out the back window. A van decorated with colorful flowers was parked next to my car.

The girl photographer opened the back door and the stretcher was placed inside. One of the young men in an orange teeshirt hopped into the back and the other sat behind the wheel. The forensic doctor got in on the other side. Before they left, the doctor had a short conversation with the long-haired lad. I watched the van until it turned at the end of the street. The commissioner's four associates did not approach the car where we were sitting, but stayed in the parking area. They looked like a group of young people cheerfully chewing the fat. If anyone had observed them just then, there would have been nothing to indicate what they'd been doing a little while ago.

As I sat back down on the seat, I slid my hand over my pants pocket, hoping this inconspicuous movement would escape the commissioner's attention. The little black telephone was still there, although in terms of security, my pocket could not be compared to the Agency's safe.

"That reminds me," said the commissioner, motioning his head in the direction the van had taken. "There's something else besides the telephone's disappearance that leads to the conclusion we're facing crossing realities again. An autopsy was performed on Miss Aksentijević's body. What do you think was the cause of death?"

I shook my head. "I don't know."

"There was no medical cause. I'm convinced it will

be the same with Inspector Vesić. We'll know soon enough."

"How can there be no cause?"

"Just like there wasn't in the 'Last Book' case. Not a single secret society, regardless of how powerful, would be able to kill without leaving at least some trace."

"But there's no mysterious book here."

"Everyone is looking for a mysterious manuscript."

"No one's found it yet."

"Who knows? That's my main problem. I don't know enough. I would certainly have an easier time if you told me what you're hiding."

He looked me straight in the eye. Just as on that morning when we stood next to the easel, it wasn't easy to bear up under such close scrutiny.

"Why would I hide something from the only person who can protect me now that I'm in the greatest danger? I'm the only one left of the three suspected of getting their hands on the Grand Manuscript."

The commissioner sighed again. "All right, if that's the way you want it, then I have no choice. The best way to protect you is to take you off the case."

"Only my superior can do that." I knew, of course, that this was useless, but frustration made me talk back.

"Don't be ridiculous. I'll take your superior off it too. This is no longer a case for the police. Actually, we should have taken it over last night as soon as the telephone appeared, and not allowed someone to nose around the Agency's safe. It was a mistake to believe that we would cooperate this time."

"You'll be making an even bigger mistake if you keep me off the case. You said just a moment ago that everything might be revolving around me again. Remember the drawing."

"That might be true, but I can't take the risk. Regrettably, I don't have full confidence in you. Good-bye, Inspector Lukić."

"Good-bye," I replied gloomily after a slight pause. I turned and started to open the door, but was stopped by his voice.

"If you want, we could take you somewhere secure until this is over."

"Thank you, but I wouldn't be secure with you even if you locked me in your safe."

Without waiting for his reply, I got out quickly and slammed the door harder than necessary.

My leaving the car seemed to be a signal for the commissioner's four associates. They left the parking area hurriedly. As they were getting into the red car, the photographer flashed me a smile. In my dismal mood, I couldn't smile back at her.

I remained beside the building entrance after the Agency car's rapid departure. The tranquil summer afternoon that suddenly reigned around me was exactly contrary to everything that had happened since I had first arrived there the night before. This peace, however, was not destined to last long. My service cell rang in my jacket pocket.

"They just called from the Agency," said Chief Inspector Đorđević. "I'm really sorry about Vesić. Did he have any close relatives?"

"Not as far as I know."

"A blessing in disguise. The hardest thing for me is notifying the family."

"Are our hands completely tied? Vesić deserves better than to have us sitting on the sideline just watching."

"I'm aware of that. I'll try to work something out. Don't do anything until I contact you. The best thing would be to come to headquarters. We've got to devise a plan and you shouldn't be alone after what just happened."

"All right."

Just as I started for the parking area, I suddenly felt weak. I turned around in confusion, but everything still looked normal. If my stomach hadn't started growling, something might have crossed my mind that was not in the least to Occam's liking.

I consulted my wristwatch: three minutes to five. It was Saturday, so it would certainly be some time before Chief Inspector Đorđević got in touch with the people who could give us back at least partial command of the investigation into Inspector Vesić's murder. For the first time since the previous night, I was not in a hurry. Finally I had opportunity to catch a bite to eat.

But where should I go? I didn't know the neighborhood well enough and there was no one around to ask. Then it dawned on me that I did know of a place. Indeed, they wouldn't serve me lunch, but I dared to hope for a sandwich. In addition, someone I would enjoy chatting with was supposed to be there from five onwards. Unofficially, of course, since the case had been taken away from me.

I headed for the teashop at a slow pace.

∽ 34 ∾

I STOPPED WHEN I reached the streetlight next to a linden tree. The night before, heading to the teashop for the first time accompanied by Miss Aksentijević, that's where I'd glanced up at the four windows of the apartment in which the writer Jelena Jakovljević had allegedly been locked. There had been a weak glow in the second window from the end. Later, as we were coming back from the teashop, none of the windows had been alight.

If that had been the end of it, I would have trusted Occam. No one could have entered the apartment until Inspector Vesić removed the key from the front door lock that had been locked from the inside. The weak glow that seemed to come from the large room was probably the reflection of some light in the street that had disappeared in the meantime. Nevertheless, it was only one in a series of illusions that Occam had not properly explained to me.

It had all started in the elevator. I had ridden in elevators lined with mirrors before, of course, but never felt as disconcerted as in this one. Its effect on me the night before had been so shattering that I dreamed about it. What had upset me the most, however, was that morning's illusion as I went up by myself to the on-site investigation after the break-in. The elevator seemed to move so slowly that I thought I would never reach the fifth floor.

And then there was the stairwell. My automatic counter had never let me down, but now it appeared to be broken. Not once had it counted the number of stairs correctly. Not only in this building but in the one where Miss Aksentijević lived as well. I had not reached the right number here until I counted the stairs to myself, accompanied by Commissioner Milenković, after the literary agent's body was found.

The most unusual illusion had taken place in the stairwell too, but it had nothing to do with counting. Miss Aksentijević and Inspector Vesić were taking the elevator up to the fifth floor and I was going on foot so we would not be too cramped together. The lights had gone off between the third and fourth floors. In the darkness I'd had the almost palpable impression of someone passing by me on their way down. But when I'd rushed to the ground floor no one was there.

Probably under the influence of my dream where everything that happened the previous night seemed strangely connected, when the elevator finally stopped on the top floor after its seemingly endless ascent that morning, I'd wondered whether something connected these illusions too. I could not detect any link between them and there had been no time to go into the matter in detail. I was still haunted, however, by the feeling that some connection existed and was even simple, and yet it continued to escape me.

I raised my head again toward the windows in the upper left-hand corner of the building. Just as in the morning, they were filled with brightly reflected sunlight, except it was now coming from the western half of the sky. As I started to lower my eyes, I thought I caught a glimpse of light movement. It was the second window again. I quickly reexamined it, but everything was now at rest.

I stood there staring a little longer, then shook my head. The play of sunlight on glass is capable of creating such chimeras, particularly if a person is inclined to see them. I headed toward the teashop, but had barely taken a few steps when I stopped dead in my tracks. That which had been persistently evading me suddenly exploded before my eyes.

The connection between the illusions was indeed quite simple, but, just as with the ducky, I had missed the obvious. They were linked by the fact that only I had seen them. There was no other eyewitness, even when someone was next to me, like Miss Aksentijević the night before on this very spot.

I had been alone in the elevator that went up at a snail's pace, alone on the stairs as my automatic counter wrongly counted them, alone in the darkness between the floors when I clearly felt someone pass by me. And I was alone right then, when something had seemed to move briefly behind the window up there.

Occam would have declared this pure coincidence. That would indeed be the simplest explanation. There was, however, another more complicated one that was not to be rejected simply because it was not to Occam's liking. A year and a half ago this world had stopped conforming to his principles and I was the last person with the right to close his eyes before the possibility that realities were in fact crossing again.

That possibility had plainly to be taken into account from the moment I, of all inspectors, stood in front of the door to an empty apartment locked from the inside, and particularly after the appearance of the telephone that worked without a SIM card and battery and that had until recently been receiving impossible SMS messages sent to me—both in terms of the speed of reply and their content.

I'd refused to accept that possibility, even though it had inevitably crossed my mind right away. I'd been devising increasingly intricate hypotheses, rejecting the one that, in spite of its complexity, was the most elegant and fully explanatory. I had even let Commissioner Milenković take the case away from me just so as not to corroborate what he had also realized—that the writer of *The Last Book* was magically influencing our reality once again.

I'd acted that way because I trusted the writer's promise that he would never do it again. The six corpses in our reality that *The Last Book* had left behind were too heavy a burden on his conscience and he could find no redemption. In addition, there was a secondary reason for not returning to our world. He never wrote sequels to his works.

Well, I could avoid it no longer. I finally had to reconcile myself to the fact that he had broken his promise; the writer was back, he was pulling strings from behind the scenes and his impact was leaving behind more corpses. I could not imagine why he was doing it. I'd been convinced that I knew him well, almost as well as I knew myself, but I had clearly misjudged him.

First of all, it was not like him to treat me this way. He had given me a thoroughly hard time in *The Last Book*, but I'd still enjoyed his goodwill. Now, however, he had started playing with me. Not out of ill will, admittedly, but he certainly must be taking pleasure in it. My conviction, for example, that I was exchanging

SMS messages with a woman must have greatly amused him. Even now, considering who was the person I had taken to be Jelena Jakovljević, it was still hard to believe that I had spoken to a man.

The illusions were playing with me too. All of this was a novel to him, a novel that would be lacking nothing if he left out the illusions that I alone knew were there. He had nevertheless introduced them to confuse and bewilder me, to put me in an awkward position. He had clearly enjoyed this, not caring whether it would confuse his readers as well. This, too, looked to me more like a female than a male trait.

I was yanked out of my musing by barking somewhere in front of me. I glanced toward the corner where I had seen a German shepherd similar to Adam that morning, but no dog was there now. I looked around me. The short street was still empty. I stood there perplexed for a moment and then it dawned on me. Another illusion! It was the right moment. I was all alone.

Or maybe not. Maybe this was a call to hurry to the teashop. There was no more time for games. The illusions were over. The novel's dénouement could not be far off. The only thing left to explain was why the writer had returned to this world.

⌒ 35 ⌒

I WAS GREETED BY the teashop's habitual gloom, so I stayed near the door until my eyes had adjusted. It took some time for my pupils to dilate, since they had completely contracted in the bright afternoon sun. Gradually I could make out parts of the underground room filled with densely interwoven herbal fragrances and the muted sounds of a stringed instrument.

Just as in the morning, the man in a white shirt and brown vest was working behind the bar. Even though the entrance was poorly lighted, he recognized me at once. He waved coquettishly. I replied by raising my hand briefly and then looked over to the other side. The patrons' contours were outlined on the banquettes along the window wall and on the nearby chairs. It seemed quite full. The only free table was the one where I had sat the previous two times.

Before heading there, I looked around the rest of the teashop, my eyes having finally adjusted. Almost all the places were taken along the two side walls as well. This time it certainly could not have been an illusion because the crowd of customers was audible as well as discernible. The din overpowering the soft music had seemed to subside for a moment as I entered.

As soon as I sat down, the curly-headed proprietor came up to me, swinging his hips.

"Welcome, Inspector! How nice to see you again."

"I didn't expect there to be such a crowd already at five."

"It's always like that on Saturday. You need a reservation." He smiled. "But that, of course, does not apply to you. Whenever you come, this table will be at your disposal."

I had to smile in return.

"Might I ask you one other favor?"

"Whatever your heart desires, dear Inspector! Just say it!"

"I'd like a bite to eat. Would you be so kind and make me a sandwich?"

"But of course! With pleasure! What kind of sandwich would you like?"

"It makes no difference. . . ."

"Come, now. Your kind of man must not be indifferent about what he eats. You could ruin yourself with the wrong food. Would you let me prepare you a special tailor-made sandwich?"

"I didn't know there were tailor-made sandwiches too."

"That's because we haven't spent much time together. Otherwise you'd know that a lot of other things are tailor-made. Particularly for you."

I cleared my throat. "Is your sister here? I can't see well in such dim light."

"Not yet, but I expect her any moment. There's just enough time for you to have a snack."

I nodded. "Very well. Thank you."

"By the way, when I talked to her on the phone, I told her that even the tea I made for you this morning hadn't got rid of your illusions. She sent word not to worry. As soon as she comes, she'll make you some tea that will get rid of all your troubles, not only your illusions."

"Tea like that would be very useful to me right now. Although the only thing she won't have to get rid of is the illusions. They're gone."

"What's that you say? So that means my tea did the trick after all, although with some delay. That's wonderful! Just leave things in my capable hands, Inspector. You have no idea how pleased you'll be."

I cleared my throat again. "What would please me the most right now is a sandwich."

"Oh, how thoughtless of me!" He tapped his forehead lightly with his fingertips, throwing his head back a little. "Here I am talking on and on, and you're dying of hunger. I'll get right to it. In a jiffy. Would I let my favorite inspector suffer?"

He turned on his heel and hastened friskily to the bar.

As I watched him busily making sandwiches, I wondered whether there were any people from the Agency among the indistinct figures in the gloom around me. The fact that the commissioner had taken me off the case did not have to mean he was no longer interested in me. He could use me as bait.

When the mysterious telephone disappeared from the Agency safe, it had become a much greater problem than the Grand Manuscript secret society. The awareness that realities were crossing once again had taken the limelight away from the fact that we were also dealing with a group of dangerous and very skilled lunatics who had already killed two people.

In the red car Commissioner Milenković had told me he would take care of them, but I thought he underestimated them. They had already outwitted him several times. If he wanted to beat them at their own game, he had to keep me in sight because he knew the secret society would be looking for me.

I was the only one left of the three who had been suspected of getting hold of the *Find Me* manuscript. If something happened to me too, the commissioner might lose his last chance to strike back at those who'd had the audacity to ridicule the Agency. And his pride.

No one had entered the teashop after me, but that didn't mean anything. The commissioner knew that I'd been here before and might even know that I'd said I would be back again after five, and sent his people in advance. They would not have needed a reservation. I started looking around slowly, hoping to make out younger, casually dressed customers, but couldn't see through the semi-darkness.

"Here's your pick-me-up!"

I turned back swiftly. Had it been the proprietor's sister, I certainly would have heard her approach, but his soft footsteps were almost inaudible. He set down a plate in front of me with two large sandwiches and a brown napkin.

"Thank you."

"But I must warn you. Once you've tasted my sandwiches, you will never think of any other."

I waited a while for him to go away, but he was clearly determined to wait and see how delighted I was with the sandwiches. I smiled graciously, picked up one and took a bite. Since I was hungry, it did me good, of course, although it did not seem out of the ordinary.

I recognized the flavors of tuna, mayonnaise, hard-boiled egg and lettuce. Had I been allowed to choose, I would certainly have left out the mayonnaise and added a bit of lemon juice, but nit-picking was clearly out of the question.

"Excellent," I said, after chewing and swallowing my first bite. I hoped my voice sounded sufficiently delighted. His face lighted up in return. I once more waited briefly, but I seemed fated to have an audience until I finished my meal. I sighed and picked up the sandwich again.

I had almost brought it to my open mouth, when my hand froze. I didn't understand what was happening at first. I wanted to finish the movement, but someone seemed to be preventing me, holding back my hand. There was no one next to me, however, except the teashop proprietor who was watching me, a smile glued to his face.

I did my utmost to get my hand moving again, but it was no good. It hung stiffly in the air, holding the sandwich next to my mouth. I was filled with confusion, having no idea what had come over me or what to do. Great willpower was needed to maintain even a little composure. First I tried to help myself with my other hand, but it lay there in my lap, also inert.

That's when panic seized me. The urge to jump headlong away from the table overcame me and when I realized I couldn't move a single part of my body, I became frantic with fear. All I could do was sit there, paralyzed, staring straight ahead while my heart pounded in my ears.

Several eternally long moments passed in this way, and then the teashop proprietor leaned toward me and stroked my cheek.

"I warned you, my dear Inspector, that after my sandwiches there would be no others."

THE TEASHOP PROPRIETOR LOOKED at me for a moment, smiling triumphantly, then moved to the left and disappeared from sight. My hearing was still good, but his movements were so quiet that I couldn't tell whether he had moved off or was still close by. I sat facing a corner of the teashop so my field of vision was quite narrow. Most of the underground room was behind my back.

The first thing I did was swear at myself for having ordered a sandwich. Even though I'd been really hungry, I should have waited a little longer. And then I realized that it really made no difference what I ordered. Whatever was in the sandwich could have been put into anything else. Into tea that removes all troubles, for example.

I had acted incautiously even though alarm bells should have gone off the night before as soon as this turned out to be a teashop and not a café, as I'd first thought. Being wary of all places like this just because of what had happened to me in the Mandarin Teashop would be paranoid, but I should not have been completely nonchalant either, particularly since I had reason to be suspicious.

First of all, such gloom where the other guests are barely visible is not the customary atmosphere for a teashop. In addition, I had been recognized as an inspector with an affinity for literature, allegedly by the way I drank tea. Finally, mentioning Jelena Jakovljević's new novel led to an invitation to come here again.

The night before I had not succeeded in talking to the woman who owned the place about these things and today I had only come across her brother. If he was her brother. And if he was the type of person he was making himself out to be. If he wasn't, then he was an excellent actor. The goodwill he showed me had appeared quite genuine. So genuine that I had actually made his job easier. Instead of refraining from ordering anything, it was I who had asked him for a sandwich—and given him a chance to put in it what they had previously given to Miss Aksentijević and Inspector Vesić.

It had probably not gone as smoothly with them as it had with me. Signs of resistance had been found in Miss Aksentijević's apartment and Inspector Vesić was not the type to give up without a fight. I, however, had played into their hands. It was almost as though I'd been cooperating. I'd already been reproached several times that day for being credulous and here I was doing it again. And at the most badly chosen moment.

Whatever they'd given me had caused no more than complete paralysis for now. There was no pain or even discomfort. After the initial shock had passed, my heart beat normally again and my breathing was regular. Nevertheless, I had no idea what might happen next. Would the effects of what I'd been given stay painless until the end? Judging by the appearance of those who had not survived the test, they hadn't seemed to suffer, but the death mask could have erased their final agony.

Although it should have been the last thing on my mind, it occurred to me that Commissioner Milenković had wrongly concluded that crossing realities were to blame for the two new deaths. The secret society had outsmarted him there too. They had clearly found some substance that kills without leaving any trace. Or at least the very sophisticated equipment at the Agency's disposal had been unable to find any trace.

Someone approached me on my left. From the heavy footsteps I knew it was the shot putter before she entered my field of vision. She paused and examined me briefly.

"I'm sorry, dear Inspector, that you didn't have a chance to try my tea against all troubles. Miss Aksentijević and Inspector Vesić were delighted. Now they no longer have any worries. But sandwiches provide much the same relief. It just takes them a little longer to kick in. I hope you'll be patient."

She turned around and headed back the way she'd come and another woman appeared from the same direction. I had to make an effort to recognize her. Although only eight hours had passed since I'd seen Mrs. Sokolović, so many things had happened in the meantime that it seemed our sole encounter had taken place long ago.

"If it made any difference, dear Inspector, I would advise you not to take at face value what the support staff say. Be wary in particular of harmless-looking cleaning ladies. You have no idea what they're capable of doing. Not just cleaning up messes, for example, but making them too. Without a sound."

She giggled and left my field of vision. Jovana Timotijević, attorney at law, entered it.

"If you could only see yourself, dear Inspector. You've gone terribly downhill. And everything could have been so different. Didn't I promise to repay you personally? If you'd just handed over what I asked for, I would have given you pleasure you'd never experience with any other woman. But you craved immortality. And this is where it brought you. It serves you right for not knowing your limits. As though immortality were for everyone."

She left, shaking her pretty head reprovingly, and made room for a girl I hadn't seen before. She was short with dark-blond hair and an oval face, wearing jeans and a checked cotton short-sleeved shirt. Everything was consistent with the look of Commissioner Milenković's new associates.

"Hello, dear Inspector," said the voice that I had previously heard through the gray cellphone. "We didn't necessarily have to meet under such circumstances, but you left us no choice. We had to put you to the test.

For your sake, I hope you haven't read *Find Me*. In that case, you will die soon, quickly and easily, like the other two. Otherwise you'll see for yourself—as I warned you—how unbearable hell is when it lasts forever."

She walked beyond my sight, but no one took her place. My heart started pounding again. So all that remained was a quick and easy death. I should have been happy with such an outcome, considering the alternative prospects, but somehow I was not overwhelmed with joy.

And then a new, tall figure began to fill my field of vision, this time from the right. It was completely covered by a white robe, the head bowed under the raised hood. It did not remain standing like the four women, but sat down on the chair across from me. After remaining motionless for several moments, it raised its left hand finally to the hood and pulled it back.

∽ 37 ∾

HAD MY FACIAL MUSCLES not been inert, they would have formed an expression of amazement. As it was, I just stared deadpan at the Grand Master whose face appeared from under the hood.

When he'd called me earlier that day on my private cell, I'd thought I still didn't know what he looked like, even though we'd met twice. I'd been mistaken, however, in both respects. We'd met more than twice and I knew what he looked like. I just didn't know that I knew it.

His thick salt-and-pepper hair was still pulled back in a ponytail, emphasizing his high forehead and bony face. This, along with his height, would have been enough to lend him a striking appearance—which was probably expected from secret order grand masters. But it was the bright green jade of his eyes that provided his true charisma.

His gaze appeared even more surreal thanks to the fact that even now, when he no longer had to pretend he was a blind painter, I couldn't tell for sure whether or not he could see. His eyes didn't seem perfectly focused on mine, but at the same time they seemed to penetrate much deeper than I found comfortable.

"Dear Inspector Lukić," he said in the voice that I'd first heard the night before in the dark corridor outside the painter Teodosijević's apartment, after Adam had growled at Miss Aksentijević and me.

I was unable to respond to his words with a bewildered expression, but this wasn't necessary. Even without it he knew he had bewildered me, so he repeated himself.

"Dear Inspector Lukić." This time his voice had the distinctive depth that I remembered quite well from the amphitheater underneath the villa where the Last Book followers had gathered. He'd spoken to me in the same voice on the telephone around three hours earlier.

"Which one do you prefer?"

He waited a bit.

"Please don't hesitate. Even though I personally like this deep voice better, I'll be happy to use the other one if you prefer."

He fell silent again for a moment.

"Oh, yes, I almost forgot. How thoughtless of me. You're not in a position to reply. You are completely paralyzed. Not much fun, is it?"

He frowned and shook his head, ostensibly sympathetic.

"Nevertheless, since it doesn't hurt, it's not so terrible over the short haul. But just imagine having to stay in that position for a long time. A very long time. Forever. Soon you'd want only one thing—for death to come and put an end to your suffering. And there is no death in deathlessness."

He paused as though wanting to let me imagine this as vividly as possible.

"And then again, perhaps you aren't facing that ghastly end at all. Perhaps you weren't lying when you said you hadn't even seen the Grand Manuscript. Ah, if only I dared trust your word. Or if another test existed, just as reliable as this one, that you would be able to survive. There is none, unfortunately. I know you'll have a hard time accepting death if you told the truth, but it is the only thing that can get you out of this paralysis. Nothing else. The immortal would envy this privilege."

He raised the left sleeve of his robe and looked at his watch.

"Just a little longer and we'll find out whether you read *Find Me*." He smiled. "It's too bad you can't speak. I'm sure that even now you'd like to satisfy that inspector's inquisitiveness of yours. It's not hard to guess which questions intrigue you. What, for example, did we give the three of you that leaves no trace? How did we intercept police communications? How were the two bodies put into the elevator? How did I disappear from a building that was under Agency surveillance? And you might also be interested in some questions that Commissioner Milenković doesn't care much about. What, for example, was in Inspector Vesić's briefcase? Do I know who the ninth Jelena Jakovljević is? Or am I really blind?"

Just then the jade needles that were aimed a little below my eyebrows seemed to plunge into my pupils.

"But we don't have time for the answers, dear Inspector. Only a few moments are left. And what would be the sense in replying if you are just about to die? If, on the other hand, it turns out that you're immortal, I'll have plenty of opportunities to reveal all the secrets to you. You'll have far more time on your hands than you want."

A veil of silence, heavy with expectation, seemed to fall over the teashop.

If I hadn't been completely paralyzed, I would have jumped up from my chair when a vibrating suddenly started in my right pants pocket.

✑ 38 ✐

IF ONLY I WERE able, I would have laughed at my predicament. There could hardly be a worse moment for a message to arrive. Just a few instants separated me from death and I couldn't move a finger. The writer had clearly lost control of what he was writing if, under the circumstances, he expected me to take out my cell and read his SMS. To say nothing of the fact that I was surrounded by an entire entourage of unkindly disposed Grand Manuscript adherents. As if I were standing in front of a firing squad just waiting for the order "Fire!"—and asked them to delay the barrage a moment or two so I could check the writer's important message.

That's when the ringing started. It didn't sound muffled in the dead silence of the teashop, even though it was coming from one of my pockets. I couldn't tell which one right away or recognize the telephone by its ring. Another amusing thought crossed my mind. If all four telephones sounded at the same time, the situation would become really grotesque. If the writer had decided to rescue me and this was all he could think of, then I didn't stand a chance and neither did his book.

The other three cellphones kept silent, however, while the fourth one rang without letup. I finally realized what would never have escaped my attention if I'd had the slightest presence of mind. But who can keep their cool when they are about to die? I didn't recognize the sound because I'd never heard it before. That telephone had only received SMS messages until now.

This realization was accompanied by another, also belated. The vibrating of the small telephone in my pants pocket had been inaudible and imperceptible to other people, but everyone had to hear the ringing. I didn't know, admittedly, about those outside my field of vision, but the Grand Master seemed completely unaware of it. Or, if he was, he was totally uninterested. His eyes were fixed on me, his expression unchanged.

And then I did notice a change. It was elusive, but certain. The green jade had lost its brightness. The needles were still there, but dulled. They could no longer penetrate inside me. It was like having a picture of the Grand Master in front of me instead of himself in person. And that's when it struck me what had happened.

No one but me heard the ringing because time had stopped for everyone else just before the first ring. Just as it had stopped for the Grand Master and the Last Book adherents, and for Commissioner Milenković and his people, in the two rooms off the corridor that linked realities. Just as it had stopped for Vera in the Mandarin Teashop as she was raising a cup to her lips from the saucer on the table.

So the writer had not lost control of what he was writing after all.

And yet, why had he let time flow for me alone when I was hopelessly paralyzed and it served no useful purpose? What was the sense of me alone hearing the ringing when I couldn't answer the telephone? None, of course, but the cell rang another three times before the scales suddenly fell from my eyes.

The first thing I did when I realized I was no longer immobile was to throw away the sandwich that had almost cost me my life. It was a reflex; I didn't intend to hit the Grand Master, although I certainly had reason enough. The sandwich hit him in the chest and fell apart, leaving a large stain on his immaculate white robe.

Then I got up briskly from the table, causing the chair to overturn behind me. I reached for the telephone as I rose, but the ringing stopped just as I stuck my hand in my right pocket. I muttered a curse and then took out the cell. There was no sign on the screen that someone had just called. My thumb hastily pushed the button to open SMS messages.

"Left of the bar. Behind the plush curtain. Door. Hurry!"

Clutching the telephone in my hand, I turned around without a moment's hesitation—and came face to face with a forest of tightly packed statues. The brother and sister, cleaning lady, lawyer and girl who called me on the gray cellphone were in the front row. Their empty eyes were trained on the place where I'd been sitting. Behind them, around thirty figures in brown robes filled the central part of the teashop. All their hoods were raised. I hadn't heard when they'd got up and gathered behind my back.

I couldn't make my way through this crowd, so I circumvented it, going between the now empty banquettes along the right-hand wall and the little round tables. No one was sitting in the chairs around them either. On reaching the bar, I ran to the other end. I didn't see the plush curtain until I got there. Even though this part of the teashop was slightly better lit, the dark-brown drape was hard to detect because it blended in with the wall of the same color.

I had already stretched out my hand to pull it aside, when I saw that not everyone was gathered in the middle of the teashop. A young couple was seated in the last two places in the left-hand corner. Peering through the semi-darkness wasn't easy even from this close. I recognized the young man first by his long hair. I had to take a step forward to make sure that the girl next to him was the photographer. And another to identify what was on the plates in front of them.

Two sandwiches. With bites in them.

Blind with rage, I spun around toward the statues.

Everything suddenly left my mind except the desire to grab the remains of the sandwiches, go back to the table where I'd sat and stuff them into the Grand Master's and brother's mouths.

The telephone's sharp ring snapped me out of my rage. Biting my lower lip until it hurt, I pulled the curtain, took hold of the doorknob, opened the door with a jerk and walked through it.

∽ 39 ∾

THE RINGING STOPPED THE instant I closed the door behind me. I was in a narrow passage that curved to the right after six or seven meters. The walls, floor and ceiling were lined with the same dark-brown plush as the curtain. The lighting was muted, with no visible source, as though the plush itself was shining.

The SMS had given no instructions about what I should do once I got there, but this wasn't necessary. There were only two possibilities—stay by the door or head down the passage. The former seemed pointless, so I started to run, although I didn't actually know why I was in such a rush.

The message had said "Hurry!" I'd even been warned by renewed ringing not to dawdle when tempted to retaliate for the murder of Commissioner Milenković's two young associates. Particularly the photographer. But no explanation had been provided.

After the curve, the passage ran straight for a dozen meters, followed by another bend, this time to the left. After I'd run along that part, I saw that the passage didn't turn anymore. It stretched out before me straight as an arrow. I might have been able to make out the end if the lighting had been better, but as it was, it seemed to stop somewhere in the distance in an indistinguishable dark point.

After I'd run another thirty meters, a door appeared

on the right. Were it not for the round doorknob, I probably would have missed it because it looked like part of the wall. I didn't become aware of the rectangle, its edges barely outlined, until I stopped.

Suddenly knocking was heard. I stared at the door in confusion, not realizing at first that the sound was coming from the inside. When it was repeated, something tempted me to open it, but another sharp ring from the cellphone put me off. One ring was enough to get me running again.

I came across another door about thirty meters further on. I could hear music before I reached it: a violin, double bass and oboe. The music grew louder and the beat quickened. As I reached the door, the composition was rising to a crescendo. I had slowed down a little before, but this spurred me to go faster.

After another thirty meters the phone in my hand suddenly rang again. I stopped and looked in bewilderment, first at the right-hand wall, then at the left. I couldn't see the outline of another rectangle or anything else unusual. The ringing didn't stop, however, until my thumb almost pushed the call button.

In the silence it left behind, I first heard a commotion from somewhere behind me and then rapid movement. People were rushing toward me from that direction. The chase was joined by a dog, who barked angrily. So that was the reason to hurry. The writer hadn't been able to keep the Grand Manuscript adherents paralyzed in timelessness for long. I ran as fast as my legs could carry me.

I didn't turn around to check and the sounds didn't confirm it, but I had the impression that they were gaining on me. I thought of drawing my gun, but it wouldn't have done much good. Even if I were to shoot the dog and hit the legs of the five or six who were heading the chase, the others wouldn't be discouraged, but enraged even further. I was being hounded by more than thirty fanatics and I didn't have enough bullets for them all.

When the end of the passage finally came in sight, panic seized me. I'd had no idea what I would find there, but it hadn't crossed my mind that there would be nothing. The passage seemed simply to end in a bare wall.

Having no choice, I kept running frantically in that direction. It was only after I'd covered half the distance to the end of the passage that I detected something on the wall after all. A black iron ladder was attached to the middle, reaching from floor to ceiling. I couldn't see where it led, but it certainly had to go somewhere. I didn't suppose it would be there otherwise.

I couldn't figure out what was on the ceiling even when I reached the bottom of the ladder. Raising my head apprehensively, all I made out was a square outline measuring one meter at most. Regardless of what was up there, it was the only place I could hope to find refuge, so I grabbed hold of the rungs.

I reached the top in an instant and did the only thing I could. Holding the highest rung with my left hand, I placed the palm of my right hand in the middle of the square and pushed as hard as I could. At first it seemed as hopeless as trying to move the entire ceiling.

Then the side next to the wall budged a tiny bit, so I quickly moved my palm to that side—and everything became easier. The hatch swung upwards. Without a second thought about what was above me, I scrambled up the last rung, climbed through the opening and stepped aside to lower the hatch as quickly as possible.

Once the hatch was in place, I almost jumped on it, convinced that no one down below could handle my eighty-five kilos, even with the strength that fanaticism gave them. That didn't seem enough, however, so I crouched down, as though this would increase my weight.

As soon as the hatch covered the opening, I was

hemmed in by darkness. When weak light had shone from down below for a moment, I'd been completely preoccupied with trying to thwart my pursuers and hadn't looked around to see where I was. Now I had no chance. All I could do was breathe heavily and stare into the impenetrable darkness, trying to figure out what to do. I kept my ears pricked too, but there was nothing to hear. The silence seemed more ominous than if a noisy crowd down there was striving with might and main to get through.

Suddenly I realized that the solution lay in my hand. All I had to do was push a button on the black cellphone. The screen would turn on and lessen the darkness somewhat in my immediate vicinity. But my thumb was not destined to complete the movement this time either. Before it could reach a button, I felt that whatever place I was in had started moving upward. And that's when I knew where I was, even though I still couldn't see.

I should have figured out where the passage was heading, of course, but the circumstances had disconcerted me completely. A mere ten minutes ago I'd been about to die, and had then rushed headlong before my pursuers. Commissioner Milenković was right. There was a secret entrance into the building at 12 Oak Street. The Grand Master had used it last night to leave without being seen. Miss Aksentijević's and Inspector Vesić's bodies had been taken from the teashop, where they hadn't survived the test, along this underground passage about 150 meters long and finally through the opening in the elevator floor, hidden by thick carpeting, where I was now crouching.

I had no time to wonder why the elevator had started moving because the carpeting began to shine at the same moment. The radiance was blue and wavering, as though I were standing on rippling water, but the unchanging firmness of the floor told me this was just an optical illusion. It lasted just as long as it took to go from the ground floor to the second floor, then was transformed into the lively glow of a fire. For a moment I had the eerie feeling that intense heat had erupted down there. But the third floor soon arrived with a new change. The fire seemed to go out and I was surrounded by darkness again, but when the flames faded from my eyes, I became aware of a weak brown glow, as though loose soil under my soles had just been touched by the dawn. The floor began to shine once more after the elevator left the fourth floor. The blueness seemed again to announce water, but it thinned and acquired a celestial translucence before the fifth floor.

Lights came on as the elevator stopped, bringing relief. Even though I knew that it had been just a chimera, the final change in the floor had frightened me. Neither water, fire, nor earth had been as scary as the abysmal empty air beneath me. The firmness of the floor had no longer been able to assure me that I wouldn't plunge from the sky.

The lights returned the carpeting to its dark-red color, but brought a new nightmare as well. I became aware of it as I rose from my crouch. I was facing toward the wall right of the door. I should have seen my reflection, but it wasn't there. As though I wasn't in the elevator, it reflected nothing but the opposite mirror, creating the illusion of infinity.

Terrified, I turned left to the wall facing the door, but I didn't see myself there either. I already knew the same thing would happen with the other two mirrors, but even so I made a quick semicircle in disbelief, stopping in front of the door. Nothing I'd seen earlier in the elevator, whether awake or asleep, had filled me with such horror as this absence of any reflection whatsoever.

If the doors hadn't opened, I wouldn't have been able to stop myself from screaming. As it was, I burst into the corridor but didn't have the courage to turn around even when I clearly heard the doors close behind me. I stood there a little longer to pull myself together. Then I put the black cellphone in my pants pocket and headed down the corridor to the right.

I was already at apartment 19 when I had the funny feeling that I'd missed something. I looked back over my shoulder. A good half-minute had to pass before I finally noticed what had changed. The four drawings on the opposite wall were no longer red but black, on a white background.

My heart jumped for joy as I pressed down on the door handle.

$\sim$ 40 $\sim$

WHEN I OPENED THE door, my first impression was that I was looking at an enormous black-and-white photograph of the short hall and part of the small room with its window in the background. The wealth of colors had disappeared, but not of shades. Between black and white stretched a magnificent spectrum of gray. I hesitated briefly and then stepped into the world as seen by the colorblind.

The photograph took on depth at the same moment, as though I'd entered the three-dimensional version of an old black-and-white movie. It all seemed unreal until I saw my hand on the handle of the door as I closed it behind me. Although its color was unnatural, it was no less real. No less mine.

I heard Vera before I saw her. She was sitting in front of the keyboard and monitor in the large room, typing. She must have known I'd come in, but she didn't turn around or stop writing. Her typing even seemed to speed up as I headed toward her. And my heart started pounding more quickly as I drew closer to her.

I'd imagined a reunion with Vera for an entire year

and a half, but nothing like this had ever occurred to me. Not knowing what else to do, I stood behind her and gazed at what was closest to me—her hair, its length unchanged. I never would have guessed what shade of gray corresponded to red. It was the same with her clothes. I recognized the cut of the tweed suit she had been wearing the first time we met. Now it looked almost black and I'd remembered it as dark blue.

The typing slowed and then stopped. Everything stood still for a few moments. Then I did what I'd been yearning to do for a long time. I touched Vera. I placed my right hand on the top of her head. It was a light, soft, hesitant, quizzical touch. Not until my fingers and palm felt the familiar cascade of thick hair was the doubt dispelled that my eyes had raised. Even though it was ash-colored, it was her red hair. My sense of sight was still able to deceive me, but not my sense of touch. It remained in the world of colors.

My hand slid all the way down her smooth hair, stopping on her shoulder. I squeezed it a little, wanting to let her know that it was me behind her even though, of course, this wasn't necessary. She raised her left hand and placed it on mine, as the fingers of her right hand quickly danced about the keyboard.

This didn't last long, and she finally turned her head toward me. The swarm of pale gray freckles joined together into a smile, lighting up her face. I returned her smile, but had no chance to bend down and kiss her because she turned her attention back to the keyboard and continued typing with both hands.

She soon finished and turned toward me again, motioning her head at the monitor. I looked at her confusedly for a moment and then over her shoulder at the big screen. She had used a font large enough that I didn't have to move closer in order to read the last paragraph that she wanted me to see.

She soon finished and turned toward me again, motioning her head at the monitor. I looked at her confusedly for a moment and then over her shoulder at the big screen. She had used a font large enough that I didn't have to move closer in order to read the last paragraph that she wanted me to see.

"We're still in the novel?" I asked.

She started typing as soon as I spoke. My words appeared on the monitor as soon as I said them. Then she hit the enter key and answered me in italics in a new line.

"Of course we're still in the novel. I have to finish the fortieth chapter. The dénouement is missing and it won't be a detective story without it."

"*The Last Book* ended in the fortieth chapter too."

"This is its sequel, so it's fitting for them to be the same."

I pondered this briefly. And she immediately wrote that on the screen.

"Are you just going to write? Aren't you going to say anything to me?"

"What writer talks while they're writing? But here, I'm talking to you through the monitor. I'm next to you. It's as though we're talking"

"It's not quite the same. I miss your voice." I paused, feeling a lump in my throat, then added softly, "I haven't heard it in a long time. . . ."

She raised her left hand again to mine on her shoulder and stroked it, while her right hand quickly wrote this very sentence.

"You'll hear it in a little while, as soon as the last chapter is finished."

"When I give it some thought, though, there's justice in this."

"Justice?"

"Yes. I was the one doing the writing for a long time."

"Are you thinking of The Last Book?"

"I'm thinking of all those SMS messages I sent you

from this cellphone." I patted my right pants pocket and then put my hand back on Vera's shoulder. "The writer arranged it so her messages arrived momentarily, as though she was saying them, while she had me write mine slowly like some simpleton. It's only fair that we change roles for a bit. Am I talking too fast? I'll be happy to slow down if you can't catch everything I say. . . ."

This time Vera slapped my hand.

"Don't you worry about whether I can catch your words. I don't type with just my thumb, like some people. . . ."

"Actually, that should have made me realize who I was dealing with. Only you would think of tormenting a poor inspector in that way."

"I hoped you would figure it out even earlier. But, as we know from other situations, it turned out that our poor inspector lacked insight."

"Like when?"

"Like when you received the first message. 'Find me.' That might have been the title of Jelena Jakovljević's new novel for other people, but I expected you to connect it to what I wrote you a year and a half ago, before I left. Do you remember? 'Don't look for me. I'll be in touch.' Well, I got in touch with a message that would have been perfectly clear to an insightful inspector. Unfortunately . . ."

"Luckily. . . ."

"Luckily?"

"If the uninsightful inspector had figured out who he was dealing with back then, the novel would have ended just after it began. It's unlikely there would have been any novel at all. This way you reached the dénouement in the fortieth chapter. And the dénouement has to begin precisely with that message of a year and a half ago that you mentioned. I think you owe me an explanation about it."

"I'm sorry everything turned out that way, Dejan. I knew our parting wouldn't be easy for you. It was even harder for me. But I had to go."

"I almost asked Commissioner Milenković to track you down."

"Not even he would have found me. The other reality is not in the jurisdiction of the National Security Agency."

"You've been here the whole time? In the writer's reality? For a year and a half?"

"That's how long it took me to write Find Me. *It might have taken less time if I'd had any writing experience."*

"Where did you get the idea to write a book? Let alone a sequel to *The Last Book*?"

"I asked the writer to do it, but he turned me down."

"You asked the writer? How?"

"He visited me."

I took my hand off Vera's shoulder.

"Why? What reason did he have to visit you?"

"Out of compassion. Kindness. A guilty conscience. He did me wrong in The Last Book. *He knew how I felt, and he had time for me. Work wasn't the most important thing for him, like it is for you. That's when I saw you very rarely."*

"Unlike police inspectors, writers are known for being laid back. And cunning. He refused to write a sequel to *The Last Book* just so he could entice you here."

"You have no reason to be jealous."

"I don't? He arranged it so you spent a year and a half with him here."

"Nothing happened."

"Is that so?"

"First of all, the writer isn't my type, and he's well along in his years. In addition, there's a technical barrier. You looked at yourself in the elevator mirrors on the way up. What did you see?"

"Nothing. . . ."

"Me neither. Visitors from the other reality are as real here as characters in a book. I've spent a year and a half in this world like a ghost. Visible only to the writer. But

intangible even to him. And how can you make love to someone you can't touch?"

"It's not entirely inconceivable. . . ."

"Maybe not, but there's a third reason, the most important one. I love you."

My hand went penitently back to Vera's shoulder.

"I missed you terribly all this time. . . ."

"I missed you too. . . ."

"Why did the writer refuse to write the sequel?"

"Among other things, because he's never written a sequel to his works."

"Some pretext. . . ."

"In any case, in the beginning he was vehemently against my coming here and writing it myself. We almost had a falling out. But the sequel had to be written, so in the end he had no choice if he wanted to help me."

"Why did it have to be written?"

"To show that there can be detective stories without killings. That was the only thing that might assuage the guilty conscience plaguing me. The writer maintained that such a book was impossible. I had to try and write it."

"It seems he was right. *Find Me* has just a few less killings than *The Last Book*—four."

"Four?"

"Well, Miss Aksentijević, Inspector Vesić and Commissioner Milenković's two associates—the photographer and the long-haired young man."

"Why do you think the photographer and long-haired young man are dead?"

"I saw them paralyzed in a corner of the teashop. They'd been served sandwiches, like me."

"Their sandwiches didn't contain the same thing as yours. They didn't have to be tested. It was known they'd never even been close to the Grand Manuscript. It was enough to incapacitate them temporarily until they were through with you. They might kill a police inspector, but they wouldn't have the audacity to harm Agency staff. As

powerful as the secret society might be, it would not be spared Commissioner Milenković's wrath."

"That's good to hear. The death of those two young people would be senseless. Particularly in a novel that was not supposed to have any victims."

"The death of those two young people, and particularly hers . . ."

"Excuse me?"

"Cut the act. You don't care a bit about the long-haired young man or whether the novel has any corpses. The photographer is the only one who means anything to you. You never stopped smiling at each other from the moment you first met. I just watched you flirt with her."

"What was I supposed to do—frown in return for her smiles? You leave me without a word of explanation. I have no idea where you are or whether you ever intend to come back. And you expect me to behave like a monk. Now I'm sorry for having lived the last year and a half like that."

Vera raised her left hand from the keyboard again and placed it on mine upon her shoulder. She didn't stop typing with her right hand.

"I should have suspected who was behind the whole thing when so many women started hanging around me," I continued. "You surround me with enterprising single young women and then accuse me of flirting because of two or three innocent smiles."

"Which one did you like best?"

I gave it some thought. "The only married one among them."

"Married?"

"Mrs. Sokolović."

"The cleaning lady?"

"Why are you surprised? You're in the best position to know what strange taste I have in women."

Her hand slapped me again and then returned to the keyboard.

"All right, there aren't four dead, but there didn't have to be even two. Inspector Vesić's death was completely unnecessary."

"I did everything I could to save him. I was really fond of him. It was your fault."

"My fault?"

"We've already talked about that. If you had solved the riddle of the ducky in time, Inspector Vesić would be alive. But your insight failed you there too, even though I almost ruined the novel's narrative coherence to give it a boost. I even sent you the photograph in the bathtub twice, and I shouldn't have done it at all."

"It's not fair to lay the blame on me. If you'd wanted me to be insightful, I would have been. But it suited you when I wasn't, because it's not good for inspectors to be too insightful in detective stories. The key secret must not be disclosed too early. And sometimes that comes at a high price. . . ."

"So now I'm to blame for Vesić's death. . . ."

"No you're not. I wasn't being fair to you when I said that a good writer would not be in an awkward position like you—having to choose between two evils. You were right to be offended by that. I should have said— an experienced writer. And this is your first novel. An experienced writer, however, was by your side the whole time as your mentor. He brought you into his world so you would write under his supervision and then he let you get tangled up with no way to resolve things. All we can do is speculate as to why. In any case, he's to blame for Vesić's death."

"Poor Inspector. . . ."

"By the way, what was in Vesić's briefcase? As you know, that rascal of a Grand Master didn't tell me."

"I have no idea."

"You have no idea?"

"I'm not an omniscient narrator. The novel is told in your voice. I know as much as you do."

"The readers will be disappointed. . . ."

"Whose fault is that? Why do they read detective stories where everything isn't explained in the usual way?"

"Some things have to be explained, though. Why didn't you show the writer that he was wrong to think it's impossible to write a detective story without any killings? Why did you go ahead and kill Miss Aksentijević when there was no need?"

"Yes, there was. She knew who was the ninth Jelena Jakovljević. She was the only one to see the person hiding behind that pseudonym. If she'd revealed it to you, the novel would have ended too early as well."

"She was removed so I wouldn't recognize you in her description?"

"Not me. Miss Aksentijević and I never met. She knew nothing about me or what I looked like, so she couldn't have described me."

"Then whom could she describe?"

"Come on, dear Inspector Lukić, put your insight to work. If it wasn't me, who else is left?"

I was silent for a few moments, my eyes fixed narrowly on the back of Vera's head.

"The writer?"

"The writer, of course. From the very beginning he engineered everything in our world so it conformed to my novel. First he rented an apartment on Oak Street that was almost identical to this one. For some reason that was important so that the two apartments from the two realities could be connected."

"Connected?"

"I'll get to that in a minute. Then he contacted Miss Aksentijević. He had an irresistible offer for her. He would be the author of Jelena Jakovljević's new novel. He didn't mention me so things wouldn't get too complicated, plus I'm a beginner while he is a reputable writer, and from another reality to boot. He promised her that this could be disclosed after the book came out. She was utterly delight-

ed. What a bestseller it would be once it was made public that the book was by the author of The Last Book."

"How did the secret society find out about it?"

"The writer took care of that. He had to involve them because that's how it was in my novel. He even arranged for the real painter Teodosijević to go on a trip so the Grand Master could use his apartment. He brought your drawing there to emphasize the relationship to the 'Last Book' case."

"He did a good job of drawing me."

"Not him. He's extremely untalented at drawing. He ordered the drawing to be made based on a photograph he took a year and a half ago."

"The drawing looks like I posed for it recently. It seems I haven't changed very much in the meantime. . . ."

"You haven't, thanks to your monastic life. Once the preparations were made, all that remained was the final act. The writer was allegedly writing Find Me *in the apartment on Oak Street, and his agent visited him from time to time. The manuscript was supposed to be finished on Friday evening, but when Miss Aksentijević appeared, she found the apartment locked from the inside and was unable to contact the writer through the intercom or telephone. She panicked and called the police."*

"There's something I don't understand. She presented the writer to me the whole time as Jelena Jakovljević. Wasn't she afraid I might find a man inside?"

"No, she realized that you wouldn't find anyone. That the writer was playing a game, regardless of what it was. All she cared about was getting hold of the manuscript, the rest was play-acting. She thought that the police would break into the apartment and she would be able to find it."

"While we're on the subject of Jelena Jakovljević's gender, the Grand Master made a slip-up. In front of Miss Aksentijević he said he'd seen the woman writer often. I didn't find that strange, but the agent realized at once that he wasn't who he pretended to be."

"That bought her a little time. If she hadn't been afraid of the fake painter, she would have gone back during the night to try and get into the apartment, and the secret society members would have been waiting for her and given her the test on the spot. This way, she lived several more hours."

"The Grand Master was nonetheless right when he maintained that Jelena Jakovljević hadn't left the apartment, even though it was locked from the inside. How did the writer pull that off?"

"Through the bathroom. It was one of the connections between the two realities. He went from this bathroom to the other one, and vice versa."

"How?"

"I don't know. He didn't tell me so I wouldn't be tempted to go back. I went through crises during that long year and a half. Being a writer is a very lonely job, particularly when you're in someone else's reality. But I think that the passage had something to do with the ducky. I didn't suspect that until I saw Inspector Kostić's photograph. The bathtub here has a ducky just like it."

A thought suddenly flashed through my brain that forced me to squeeze Vera's shoulder.

"Did Vesić find it out somehow . . . ?"

"Wouldn't he have told you if he had?"

"He didn't have a safe way. If realities had crossed again, every contact with me would be under surveillance. Nevertheless, he sent me a message, except I was blind to it at first, and afterward, until now, too dim-witted to interpret it properly. Turning the ducky around was not his customary sign that he'd broken into some seemingly inaccessible place, but a message about what was behind it all."

"If that's true, then we don't have to speculate as to why my mentor, as you say, let me get tangled up without a good resolution. He had to remove Inspector Vesić before the two of you met so you wouldn't find him out too soon, and I had to do the dirty work for him."

"So the writer was to blame for both murders in your novel and if we accuse him he'll invoke the book's narrative coherence, which would be jeopardized without those two violent deaths."

"I still think it's possible to write a detective story without a single murder, but also without jeopardizing its narrative coherence. If I decide to try it again, it will certainly be without a mentor. And in my own reality."

"The one mistake in narrative coherence is nevertheless your fault."

"Really? What's that?"

"Saving the main character in the teashop."

"Would you have preferred for me to let you die just for the sake of the novel's narrative coherence? In any case, there's narrative coherence of a higher order here. This novel is intended to be a melodrama, and they are the best when they have happy endings."

"So what happy ending awaits us?"

"An original one. As far as I know, there has yet to be a story written that ends like that. I was inspired by your jealousy. You suspected there was something between the writer and me. There wasn't, but at the end of this novel the writer and the main character will make love."

"The writer and the main character?"

"That's right. In this reality I'm a writer and you are a character in my novel."

"And we're going to make love in front of all the readers?"

"Don't be silly. That would be lowbrow literature. Pornography. This is a serious melodrama. We will soon exclude the readers. I can hardly wait to stop writing. It's really tiring like this."

I looked around the large room.

"Well, I don't know. I've never made love in black-and-white. . . ."

"Oh, in the end you'll see what real colors are. . . ."

Contributors

About the author

Zoran Živković was born in Belgrade, Serbia, on October 5, 1948. Until his recent retirement, he was a full professor at the Faculty of Philology, the University of Belgrade, teaching creative writing. He is one of the most translated contemporary Serbian writers: by the end of 2019 there were more than 100 foreign editions of his books of fiction, published in 23 countries, in 20 languages.

Živković has won several literary awards for his fiction. In 1994 his novel *The Fourth Circle* won the Miloš Crnjanski award. In 2003, Živković's mosaic novel *The Library* won a World Fantasy Award for Best Novella. In 2007 his novel *The Bridge* won the Isidora Sekulić award. In 2007 Živković received the Stefan Mitrov Ljubiša award for his life achievement in literature. In 2014 and 2015 Živković received three awards for his contribution to the literature of fantastika: Art-Anima, Stanislav Lem and The Golden Dragon.

Zoran Živković has been recognized with his selection as European Grand Master for 2017 by the European Science Fiction Society at the 39th Eurocon in Dortmund, Germany.

Živković is the author of 22 books of fiction:
    The Fourth Circle (1993)
    Time Gifts (1997)
    The Writer (1998)
    The Book (1999)
    Impossible Encounters (2000)
    Seven Touches of Music (2001)
    The Library (2002)
    Steps through the Mist (2003)
    Hidden Camera (2003)
    Compartments (2004)
    Four Stories till the End (2004)
    Twelve Collections and the Teashop (2005)
    The Bridge (2006)
    Miss Tamara, The Reader (2006),
    Amarcord (2007)
    The Last Book (2007)
    Escher's Loops (2008)
    The Ghostwriter (2009)
    The Five Wonders of the Danube (2011)
    The Grand Manuscript (2012)
    The Compendium of the Dead (2015)
    The Image Interpreter (2016)

About the artist

Youchan Ito was born 1968 in Aichi prefecture, Japan. She launched her career as a graphic designer in 1988, becoming a freelancer illustrator in 1991 and founding Togoru Co., Ltd. with her husband in 2000. In 2017 the company was reborn as Togoru Art Works. Handles a wide range of genres including cover art and design for science fiction, mysteries and horror titles, as well as illustrations for children's books.

www.youchan.com